HOW IT FEEDS

ELIJAH B. WILDER

HOW IT FEEDS
Elijah B. Wilder

All rights reserved. No part of this book may be reproduced in any form or by any mechanical means, including information storage and retrieval systems, without written permission from the author (except for the use of brief quotations for book review purposes).

Copyright Elijah B. Wilder, All rights reserved.

This is a work of fiction. Any resemblance to actual persons or events, living or dead, is purely coincidental. The horror you may incur, however, is real.

Cover illustration and interior formatting by Chris Krawczyk. Edited by philip rowan.

First Edition Published by Little Ghosts Books, Oct. 2025.

ISBN 978-1-0695415-0-5 (Paperback)

HOW IT FEEDS
ELIJAH B. WILDER

Content Warnings:

Substance abuse/addiction, suicide, abuse of power dynamics, institutional transphobia, redress of objectification/fetishization of trans men (cathartically redressed via fictional floral sexual violence), and aforementioned floral sexual violence.

Little Ghosts Books
Toronto, ON Canada

"Good Heavens, what insect could suck it?"

Charles Darwin, in a letter to Joseph Hooker, on the
long-spurred orchid *(Angraecum sesquipedale)*

"But if you tame me, then we shall need each other. To
me, you will be unique in all the world. To you, I shall be
unique in all the world..."
"I am beginning to understand," said the little prince.
"There is a flower... I think that she has tamed me..."

Antoine de Saint-Exupéry, *The Little Prince*

But the boy stayed away for a long time. And when he
came back, the tree was so happy she could hardly
speak. "Come boy," she whispered, "come and play."

Shel Silverstein, *The Giving Tree*

For the moth that managed to find its way into my metaphorical nectary tube and, in so doing, help me feel more at home in this spectral forest world.

Excerpt, "Introduction: A Radical
New Ethic in the face of the SMEE,"
Elegy for an Almanac: Ecology after
the Sixth Mass Extinction Event by
Leon Angelo, Ph.D. California
National University (2059)

Apollo, mourning his fallen lover Hyacinthus, at once sees his own guilt in the boy's wound while also refusing to accept responsibility for it. "Because," he asks Ovid's readers, "how can one be guilty of simply playing a game how it has always been played?"

A floral memorial, the hyacinth holds Apollo's sorrow so the god does not have to. Have we not transferred our own guilt to the natural world? Forced flowers to bear our burden for us? We do not hold this guilt. For how can one be guilty of simply playing a game how it has always been played? For living within a world of systems how they have always functioned?

What is needed if what remains of the natural world—and indeed the planet itself—is to survive is an act of radical responsibility. Not for the past that led to this unblooming present, but for the future. The question of whom to blame is ultimately a distraction. After the flowers are no longer mute, after the springs are no longer silent, then we can do the unhappy work of doling out crimes and punishments (though we will have outgrown them). We are out of time. This is a fact. We have been out of time for decades and done nothing but search out someone to blame. The way forward is simply forward *and together*. Forced atomization of our communities, both human and natural, is mirrored by the atomization of our minds. It is not enough for scientists to work with poets. Scientists must *become* poets, and poets scientists. Only then will we, as a species and member of the larger community of Earth, be able to recognize—and then contend with—the many wounds wrought by this multigenerational game we've all played. That game has no winners. We have, all of us, lost this game spectacularly.

One day did not work.

It is time for *now*.

Part I: *Kairomone*

I must look like Charon, fishing for the dead by lantern light.

Or I would if there were anything left alive to watch me. Only the bones of the forest remain. Trees... moss... lichen. Sterile white light bounces over trunks and gives shape to shadows in the night. I cast bars wherever I move—a woman, too, when my right hand gets tired and I shift the lantern to my left.

This field research grant is generous folly. There are no moths left. Not here. Even if the rumor of *Eumorpha pandorus* sightings were true, there's no way for it to survive long. All the flowers are gone. How would it feed?

My teeth chatter and I pull up my muffler. Forget sustenance. How would any moth survive *this*? The coldest Florida winter in over a century? When I entered the Western Expanse from the east, my footsteps had all been silent, muffled by soft loam. Now, all the bits of leaf and decay-moist soil have turned every step into a *crunch*. Those sounds, each an unmistakable signal of my presence, make me wary. There's no reason they should. I'm alone out here, the only animal for hundreds of miles. I dig out the gloves that will make me far less dexterous, but far less cold, and soothe myself like a child convinced there's a monster in the dark hall outside her bedroom door. How could I be anything *but* alone out here? This rare stretch of wilderness (such as it is) is completely cordoned off, jealously guarded by a government undaunted by international newsreel footage of barbed wire and guns aimed at activists.

It took two years for DTU's Natural Philosophy department to get an entry permit to chase after rumors that somewhere in this caged, naked jungle, an insect remains. Two years is about as long as anybody can hope for a Pandora to live— that was *before* the air became too thick for flying things.

What a cruel joke.

Now, backpacking through miles of too-cold and too-quiet subtropical preserved wilderness, it would seem the only one playing cruel jokes on me is *me*. There can be no one else here. That knowledge doesn't make me feel any less watched. Rationality never holds quite the same sway in the dark.

Good God, am I really crying? I rub my face, but the waterproof coating on my gloves just smears the tears across my cheekbone. *You're such a child sometimes*. I sure feel like one, because it hardly seems fair, does it? That I should feel such grief—

mourning my solitude in what *should* be a rich ecosystem teeming with life—*and* feel the uncanny sense of being watched by something living at the same time?   But rationality never holds quite the same sway in the dark.

And "fair" means nothing to a forest.

I pause, giving any sphinx moths in the vicinity a moment to catch up to my lantern light. Nothing comes but the sound of leaves rustling... branches creaking. No moths. No birds. Nothing but trees, the dark, and the shadow cage my lantern casts on the forest floor.

The last time I saw a moth in the wild was 2030. I was six. I'd shooed it off of me then, no idea I was watching something so fragile, so precious fly away. Every moth I saw outside of a lab since then has been dead... little more than tiny, crumpled paper planes on the street. Even those sightings stopped by the time I finished middle school. Dead moths heralded dead pigeons. Robins. Bluejays. Mice. Rabbits. Owls. Hawks. Foxes.

Emory was burnt to the ground not long after that, along with a dozen other universities across the South. Not because the researchers there couldn't find a solution to the Sixth Mass Extinction Event. They had. But they'd solved the wrong problem:

Human error.

We are made in God's image, the then state of Florida Governor had said. *And God doesn't make mistakes.*

He does punish the wicked, though.

My scholarly responsibilities don't disappear just because I've started spontaneously regressing in the woods. No data is still data. I clear my throat and say, "Take dictation." The voxnode stuck beneath my ear beeps twice before a feminine voice honed by decades of consumer research to sound just the right blend of competent and nonthreatening to men tells me what I already knew: "*No signal.*"

I sigh. It was glitching before I reached the Dead Zone, and that was just a local connection. Communication infrastructure isn't a priority in the Free Republic of Florida's national budget, and Californian tech's been banned for all but top government officials and their friends. Whispers in the braver halls of DTU have hinted that the Western Expanse Wilderness has proven impenetrable to even Californian tech—that no manmade signal is capable of penetrating whatever peculiar brand of wildness had been captured and contained here. There is no way for me to fall on either side of that speculation aisle. It hardly matters anyway.

The second I shift my muffler aside to enter a manual command on my voxnode, cold slips in like an opportunistic thief. "Dictation," I say. "Doctor Ismene Nakamura, Professor of Natural Philosophy and Robert F. Kennedy Chair of Wildlife, DTU. December 21st 2060. Time"—a glance at my watch—"1800 hours." Exact coordinates aren't an option, and my maps (digital or paper) are less than helpful. Best I can do is "Western Expanse, Free Republic of Florida," so I leave it at that. If I actually manage to find this insectile ghost, then I'll worry about my coordinates. "No sign of *Eumorpha pandora*."

My laugh is a weak, fleeting cloud on the air. I'm becoming everything I promised myself I wouldn't. Slapdash. Intellectually complacent. Unscientific. When the south-eastern corner of the country seceded from the rest, so many of us swore we'd stay and resist. Never give in to the impulse to go with the flow and keep from making waves. Some really didn't. Many empty chairs were left behind in the Natural Philosophy Department— along with all the benefits and protections that come with them. Their loss is a wound that will be felt for decades in this collective pursuit of human knowledge that is science.

Where would science be in this corner of the continent if we'd all made the same (ultimately futile) gesture? Buried beneath thousands of bible pages. But here, working from the inside, we can still do the real science. We can use the phraseology the DOL demands, but we know—we know—how to read between the lines of the scriptural bullshit. When we see "divine guidance," we know the scholar is discussing *evolution*. "Divine inspiration?" *Nonhuman Intelligence*. The real work is there. You just have to know how to look for it. That's why I'm here: to do the work. To *look*. This isn't a matter of publish or perish for me. Even if I never publish again, my Fidelity Ranking is plenty high enough to ensure my security at the university until retirement.

Moral purity and revolution are all well and good. Admirable. For those of us with families to support and people to lose, they're all just make-believe games with imaginary stakes played at impossible odds. We've all made sacrifices. I'm going to make sure those sacrifices *mean something*... if I have to freeze to death (in *Florida* of all places) to do it.

Even with heavier gloves, I can't feel my fingertips. I shift the lantern to my left hand. Shadow bars shuffle, then stack. *Two* silhouettes appear behind them. Mine—the *smaller* one—takes a step back.

The larger takes a step forward.

I spin around. "Who's there?"

Nothing. No one.

I resume my original position as best I can and look again. Nothing. Just the shapes of trees and my own shadow. Wind shifts the branches, and the shadows swell then contract again, creaking and undulating like an ancient ship on a frozen sea. The human eye is well honed to pattern recognition—so well honed, in fact, it will find faces where none exist. Of course a lonely human would create companions in the darkness.

I repeat this to myself three more times, but that missed-a-step catch in my chest won't go away. The mind can only do so much to convince the body. My skin's delusion that I am not alone follows me. It likely will all the way to Waypoint Four.

Night proper falls, and I still haven't reached the camp. I've got my lantern for ambient light, and a flashlight in my pocket should that fail. The halo I walk in casts the forest in almost complete darkness. The forest is so quiet, so still, so dark, the slightest deviation in that quiet, dark stillness is as good as a torch flare. My attention locks onto the barest flicker of motion to the north. I watch. Listen. Nothing, not even wind. Then, a rustle of leaves. I follow the sound, squinting into the darkness beyond my lantern's reach. As my eyes settle into that liminal space between pitch black and LED light, a form takes shape.

It moves.

A black creature, low but large and quick, weaves between larger silhouettes. Silent. Once I lose sight of its faltering silhouette, my eyes chart its most likely trajectory given its previous pace. With luck and reliable peripheral vision, I catch motion to my left, several yards farther than the thing should have been able to manage—now, just five yards separates it from me.

It moves through a sliver of moonlight: a crouched, wretched thing on all fours, long sticks for legs. It hobbles stiffly along a stuttering path from tree to tree, melting into shadow after shadow.

Circling me. Every now and then—just long enough for one quick gasp—bright yellow eyes blink at me.

A slow, deep breath. I raise my lantern high in one hand and point my flashlight with the other, chasing down the fable creature.

It's a coyote. Far, far thinner than any living, quick-moving creature ought to be. But it's a coyote. Just a coyote. Tongue lolling, legs stiffened to stilts by malnutrition. A ratty fur blanket stretched over wicker. Mottled black. Like the grumpy gargoyle of a tortoiseshell cat that used to prowl the New Jersey neighborhood my husband and I lived in before opportunity took me south. Aya, my mother-in-law, had called the cat "Sabi-san." Mr. Rust. I thought it was sweet before my husband let me know it was like naming the cat "Mr. Calico." She wasn't naming it. Sabi-san wasn't a *who*. It was a *what*.

Where did it go?

Pointing my flashlight where I'd last spotted the pitiful beast reveals nothing but a quickly fading cloud of breath. Exhausted though I am, I run the rest of the way to Waypoint Four. It must be close. It has to be. Even in this uncharacteristic cold, my khakis chafe along the waistband where sweat is soaking through. The thighs and crotch follow soon after. I don't even realize my mortifying error until I stop to relieve myself at a conveniently shaped ring of thick roots.

My request to the government for menstrual reprieve had been denied. Blood, the young cherry red of a fresh cycle, dapples the softest, palest parts of me. My thighs are bone-white on the best of summer days—even smudged in blood, they don't register as anything but *pale*. It's tacky against my fingertips. Already cold to the touch after just a few moments crouched low, pants down. Heat drips from my spine, pooling deep inside me. The way the sight of my husband taking off his belt after I'd made a mischievous little comment just to rile him up used to do to me. The way watching my father take off his belt after my brother had made a little comment just to prove he existed used to do to me.

The heat blooming between my legs feels all the hotter for the cold. I scoff at myself and press my palm against my groin. Blood drips. With every barely-there *pat* of warmth against my skin, the heat on my throat and cheeks inches higher, reaching for my eyes.

For all the paranoia that's dogged me in my solitude, I've never been more grateful to be alone. Professor Endersby had offered to join me on this excursion. He'd told me our Californian counterparts hadn't even been granted access yet, but were already training to enter the wild using sensory deprivation tanks—even periods of extreme isolation. *To test for suitability to the environment*, he'd said.

Endersby's name had disappeared from the steel plaque on his office door before I could tell him: *No, thank you. I don't mind working alone.*

The blood pooled in my palm has already begun to matte and congeal on the surface. I scrape it onto a papery length of root and pull myself together. It won't be long now. Waypoint Four can't be far.

Indeed, it is not. But God forbid the requisite supplies be waiting for me there. It takes a lot of boot-kicking and twice as much swearing to get the cache lids to give. All that effort for some water purifiers, freeze-dried gumbo, astronaut ice cream (a joke?), and a completely senseless array of tools and components—most of which are useful only for repairing the sort of equipment that isn't even allowed past the first of three checkpoints guarding the Western Expanse. The checkpoint staffed by smooth-faced men in camouflage who still find it in them to joke with one another while they march along the outermost wall. Half a mile past that, at the second checkpoint, the men stationed there don't smile. By the third and final checkpoint, they don't even make eye contact: not with me, at least. Such big imposing men with their black body armor and multiple guns strapped to their hips with another resting on their shoulders—not like a marine attending a funeral, but like a soldier expecting to use it. Then, it had been strange how they seemed so *reticent*. Of what? Of me? Of what lies beyond that twenty-foot wall of concrete, rebar, and electrified razor wire?

Now, unfurling my orange tent from its vacuum-sealed tube, I can't help but feel like I'd misread those averted faces. They weren't afraid or shy. They'd been turning their eyes away how any decent man would have done, had he stumbled his way through this wilderness to find me squatting on these roots, bare as nature. Gentlemen.

Those men weren't just being polite.

Those men were ashamed.

Again, my blood feels all the warmer for the cold. The flush to my cheeks prickles like a limb that had fallen asleep finally coming back to brilliant, thorny sensation. I've no choice but to craft my own hygiene products from first-aid supplies. I feel a bit like a scarecrow, stuffing myself full of gauze, only less lucky: scarecrows can't feel the straw scratching inside them. The blood on my fingers has dried already, making their movements stiff. I'm reluctant to replace my gloves. The thought of crusted blood smeared on the tent is far easier to stomach. Nylon cleans easier than shearling. The rain will take care of it... surely it will rain. At this point, maybe it will just *snow*? My smile, brittle as it is, chases back my rising blush.

There won't be any snow. Winter, yes, but no snow.

The temperature drops quickly once I'm set up, holed away in my solitary tent. How very polite of it. Gentlemanly. Another brittle smile, a wry laugh for none but me to lift a commiserating brow to. I'd meant what I'd said to Professor Endersby. I truly don't mind being alone. I'm not bothered by the quiet. I used to love wandering through what remained of the woods in my college days in the early hours—especially during the colder months.

Stubborn lines of dried blood remain on my hands, charting out red lines of fate from heel to fingertips. I've wasted enough cleansing cloths. Whatever won't be budged by soap and friction certainly won't be budged by casual touches of metal and plastic. I clip my small lantern to a carabiner and hang it above my head, watching it sway. Cool and sharp as that LED light is, the sight of it is warming. Like it might make puppet shows of the scarier shadows. Shame it casts no real warmth, though.

I don't think I used to mind the cold this much. Before relocating to Florida, I used to *love* winter. I loved it for how easily the wind could move. How everything else in the world being so still, so quiet, let the mumbling, whispering things be heard. There's nothing of that full stillness in my tent—only a buzzing, angry emptiness. The silence before the storm, the quiet before the snap never allowed release. There's only ever going to be quiet here, now, alone in a tent in the woods. No orchestra of bugs and frogs. No birds. No squirrels kicking up leaves with such gusto that theirs becomes the echo of an animal a hundred times their size. Sometimes wind shifts dead wood. A puppeteer. Something *living* granting the illusion of life to something *not*.

Did we appreciate just how many sounds a creaking branch could make back when there were owls and raccoons to listen for—growls to listen *out* for—instead? Up north, the water inside the trees will freeze and expand, making a high-pitched whine, slow like a hungry cat's. Spring thaw gives the wood a long, low creak. The illusion of wildlife. But not here. Here, remarkably cold though it is, nothing freezes that deep. Every sound is a moan deep from the belly of the forest. The gurgling groans of something warm and wet.

And yet, that is my breath blooming white in the lantern light. My mouthed *"Damnit"* forms another little cloud, and I wriggle deeper into my sleeping bag. Cold pins me down, makes my legs feel shorter than they are. Childlike. I only remember *remembering* losing consciousness one time: during a sleepover when I was eight. I was cold then, too. Julie's basement was freezing, and we'd only one thin sheet between us. I saw the black rising before I closed my eyes and thought how strange it was as I, a waking, living girl, could be dragged to sleep by a frozen lullaby of submission. The same one is pulling me under now.

I think how strange it is and watch, frozen, as something cold covers my eyes before I can will them to close.

Cold shakes me awake.

I reach for my phone, but my nightstand isn't there. Neither is my phone. Edges of frozen earth push up through the tent's footprint, sharp against my palm. Waking realization shifts my hand's trajectory upward to search instead for a smooth, round lantern. The carabiner above my head clinks. Empty.

My lantern isn't there.

But I hung it there. I remember hanging it there. My tablet *is* here, thank God. Anywhere but a tent in the wilderness of night, its green-haloed screen would have been pitiful light. Now it's enough to make out wrinkles in the nylon. A trick of that light turns the orange tent to a deep, dried-blood red. I shift the tablet to the other side to search out the slash of a zipper. A C-section scar bisecting the shriveled gut of a tent. The only thing letting me out (or keeping me in).

A warning beep, low and hollow.

"Damn, damn, damn!" The tablet's plugged into the power bank—like the lantern should have been—but it hasn't charged at all. Power's at less than 3%. "Damn, crap, *shit!*" I power it down to conserve what little charge is left. Again, blackness consumes me while I watch, eyes wide open.

My vision refuses to adjust after staring at a bright tablet for so long. All I see is a black so dark, my brain scrambles to break up the monotony by pasting swathes of impossible indigo—that shade that exists nowhere but the human mind—onto the places it thinks things, *anything* should go. I feel my way along nylon and pull the zipper to look out at a blackness no less monotonous, no less bruised by the illusion of difference.

Then, not just anything. *Something.* A lighthouse to focus on. A siren too jealous to let me perceive anything else. Whatever it is, it's bobbing up and down... or back and forth? No way to know where the path is going with no point of reference but *it*. But the point of brilliant, cold white *is moving*. I know that much.

That's my lantern. Has to be. The light is too blue, too clinical to be anything but an LED.

But where? Distance is meaningless in the darkness. I have no sense of scale. The light might be ten meters, a hundred meters away. Ten thousand.

When I whisper, "Fuck me," my mouth holds the final e in a chattering rictus. I pull on more layers (probably backward or inside-out) and pat around for my boots. The knife my husband made me bring is tucked in the right one. For all my grumbling and eye-rolling that distant Monday morning, I tuck the knife back in once my boots are on. The folded metal presses against my ankle, reminding me of its presence with every other step.

I'm here, Ismene, it says. *I am cold, I am hard, but I am real and I am here.*

Even as raised roots keep tripping me, my eyes never stray from the light ahead. I stumble and just catch myself on a hanging vine. The knife reminds me with its blistering kiss of steel, *I'm still here.* Cold comfort is better than no comfort at all.

Wind moves freely, uninterrupted by leaves or mountains or bodies. It's enough to push the clouds past the bottom hook of the crescent moon.

Behind me, a woman gasps.

I freeze.

She *shrieks*.

Paper rustles. Leaves? No, feathers. I feel it before I see the massive bird diving ahead of me. It's an *owl*. A barred owl. I know it from the call, but even that scant moonlight is enough to cast a shape that is unmistakably owl. The bird goes dead-silent in flight. It lands with a whimper-creak of wood above me. Feather-gloved toes flex on the branch.

"Impossible," I say. And it is. That owl can't be here. It can't survive.

What would it eat?

Another scream. The owl's cry is distressingly human and distinctly feminine. Surprised. As a child, I used to think barred owls sounded scandalized. Comical. Now, the sound pulses in the air like a physical thing that swallows every other sound around it. A crack in the ice. A shattered glass that hushes a chattering restaurant. A single gunshot silencing a classroom.

The owl fluffs its feathers and clicks its beak. Something's piqued its attention. Plumage ruffles then settles like a hundred soldiers standing at attention. White and brown, as if something had clawed through a stretch of snow, revealing furrowed brown earth beneath. Not the russet *S. v. georgica* that *could* be here. Or, could have *been* here. That bird craning its head to look straight through me is *S. v. varia*. The northern barred owl.

What does it matter? It's not as if the southern variety is any *less* impossible than its northern counterpart—or *any* counterpart. Any relative, any neighboring species... *they're* all dead, too.

The memorial echo of my sophomore-year biology teacher corrects me. *Species don't die, Ismene. They go extinct.* But if that's really true, Professor, why does this owl feel like a ghost? Why does this forest feel haunted?

Eyes, solid and black like a doll's, meet mine. There is no color there. No movement. Not so much as a twitch of beak, but the owl is crying again— stealing any and all sound from the wind, my breath, and the click of frozen mud caked in my boot tread. The call echoes somehow, and those echoes are too close. Too contained. As if the darkness were really glass, jarring us all inside.

I back away, keeping my hands stretched out around me to feel for obstacles. Doll eyes follow me, empty. Something wet brushes my cheek. Am I crying? Another wet touch to my nose, my chin. No. It's snowing.

Again, the owl cries. Again, the wind shifts. The second claw of the moon stabs through the ever-present Florida haze. Only, the moon isn't a crescent any more. It's full, round and bright. Bright enough to see that this cannot be Florida.

It cannot *be at all.*

Glittering snow lights up in a lantern unto itself, blanketing the entire forest in variegated bars of black and the peculiar, ghostly blue that white transforms into at night. Trees bleed the same black of their bark, casting shadows that leech into the snow where they're dragged on and on and on... like a word written on cotton rag only to be regretted, a mistake smeared with little success, then buried beneath a dozen ink crosses. My lantern won't be so glaring in this dim sea of blue light, but that means it isn't quite so necessary for navigation, either.

I find it anyway. Or, my foot does. The timid resistance of snow gives way to something hard and real. I unearth it like an archaeologist revealing bones, brushing away an amount of powder that can't have possibly fallen since the thing went missing. I switch it on. Its plastic housing is cracked, but the light still works. I twist the nob again.

Off.

Again.

On.

Movement.

Another flying thing? A moth? Yes, there. *Right there*, flying just close enough for me to reach out and touch—if I could only work up the nerve to free myself from this standing sleep paralysis. It can't be. *You can't be here.* And yet, *it is.*

One powder-white moth, barely the size of my thumbnail.

I am completely still. I don't even breathe. I'm too terrified my lung-filtered air might be enough to strike it dead. I will the moth away each time its flirtatious trajectory brings it closer to me, closer to this corrupting human interference in an impossible forest.

The moth only continues its scattered, connect-the-dots path before alighting upon my gloved thumb.

Fear gives way to awe, and I whisper, "My god...." My wonderment collects in a cloud of frozen breath, faint enough to dissipate in the subtle motion of tiny, weak wings.

The moth pumps its wings slowly, flattening to display the faintest striations of white before closing like a book. Now still, folded, the faint pattern dotting the undersides of its wings emerges: not bars, but perfect little silver freckles. Though, maybe not silver. It's less a color so much as the absence of one, like the eye of a needle. The moth must be warmer that way, wings pressed together like that. Should I take off my glove? Give it someplace warmer to rest? Eyes fixed upon the moth on my hand, I carefully reach out with the other to pat my pockets, hoping I wasn't so foolish, so hopeless and pessimistic as to leave camp without a specimen jar.

I was.

But the crack in the lantern is wide. This moth might fit inside. Moths are drawn to light; it's not such a bad solution. I form my hand into a loose claw and attempt to herd rather than nudge it inside the broken plastic. Its legs cling to my palm, reluctant to shift from the warmth. A cautious puff of breath ushers it off my glove and inside the lantern.

Staccato flittering makes an abstract shadow

puppet show of the forest. It isn't a sphinx. No, *this* moth is too small, too delicate—as perfectly cloud white as my incredulous puffs of laughter in the frozen air. *Hyphantria cunea.* Fall webworm.

I've never seen one before, dead or alive. It's a name I learned how children generations before me must have learned the names of constellations: as complicated nonsense names from a dead language made familiar with a picture and a story. This constellation was the story of a moth that was speckled in the south east, but perfectly powder-white in the north. It kept its family warm with lovingly spun webs hung high in the trees like gossamer castles in the sky.

Cancer killed my grandmother slowly. It gnawed at her bones, leaving behind networks of gauzy channels. Her final year was held together by plaster casts and doctor appointments. I suppose her present must have lost its reality once no future tethered it there. She only spoke of the past those last few months. I visited in the winter to bring her meals and medicines, clear away trash, and bear witness to any little relics of history. These might just as easily have been half-remembered television episodes or second-hand stories from friends as Grandma's own experiences. There was no question of this particular memory's veracity, though. It was hers. As unmistakable as knowing that the CRACK you've just heard is what a femur breaking under its own weight sounds like.

Grandma told me that her father used to

walk the yard of her childhood home in upstate New York, sawing off web-woven branches of hickory and elm as he found them. He'd shove them into a big metal can before dousing it all with kerosine and setting it on fire. She said she could hear them screaming. Her father scolded her: *it's only the water in the wood boiling, like our tea kettle.* But the little worms writhed like they were screaming. They fled from flame to flame then stopped to do nothing but writhe and wait and scream. And she would watch them. Never helping. Never thinking to. Only watching and waiting and witnessing as the trees screamed for the mute insects burning beside them.

In my own untethered present, I watch the moth throw itself against the lantern's edges. It always seems to *just miss* the cracks.

The way back to my tent is far longer than the way out here had been—wherever here even *is*. As if the path were made of taffy and I'd pulled it into a longer, thinner string behind me. An illusion, of course. I'd been running after my lantern: the chase had detonated my night with a burst adrenaline and fog.

In the stillness that's followed since, the cold hangs heavier. The fog, thicker. It *looks* cold. The ground seems to exhale along with me, venting steam. Moist air condenses and collects in a mist so fine, it's little more than distortion to my eyes, like I'm looking at the world through a smeared lens. If I were driving, I'd be using my wipers just to keep the fog at bay. But it doesn't *feel* cold, is the odd thing. It's more that I know it must be cold. Only, it doesn't *smell* cold. The air tastes wet, but not *cold.*

Perhaps there's just some unique quality to Florida cold alien to me. I've only lived here six, seven years—certainly never experienced a cold snap like this. I find myself rotating my right foot just to feel the presence of the knife in my boot.

Be objective. Step back. You are not part *of this environment. You are* observing *this environment.*

Deep breath in through the nose... out through the mouth. I bite off my glove to better access the manual controls for the voxnode behind my ear. "Dictation," I say. "Doctor Ismene Nakamura, Professor of Natural Philosophy and Robert F. Kennedy Chair of Wildlife, DTU"—I check my watch—"April 1st 2055, 16:30—"

I stop, stare. Sure enough, my watch reads: 4/1/2055. The time: 4:30 PM. Damned thing must have been affected the way that so much equipment is. The time *had* been correct earlier... though, I have no way to confirm that. Hopefully, my voxnodes are faring better. "Correction: Precise time unknown—"

Static crackles behind my ear.

I give the device a sharp tap and proceed. "I've located what appears to be—"

Crickle-crack.

Another tap, harder this time. "A specimen—*no!*"

I recoil, jump back—from what, I have no idea. The static crackle against my ear had been so sudden, so loud, it had become a physical touch. Violating. I hold my breath, listening to the muffled ocean sounds that only ever come from behind me.

Crickle...crickle-crackle-crick... "Ih—eh—ne?"

My face contorts with the effort of listening.

Crackle-hiss... "Is—Ismene?"

The world freezes over once I recognize—or, think I recognize—that voice. "What in the—"

"*Ismene-E-E-E-E!*" the final, long *E* of my name holds, rises, an unrelenting siren shrieking in my ear—from inside my ear. I claw at the voxnode, barely registering the dry *rip* of adhesive pulling from the fragile skin of my neck. It's not even halfway off when it goes quiet. The relief of silence deadens the pain, but the echo of that shrill beep vibrates still, tickling my throat like the threat of a cough.

A quiet, sibilant whisper of nonsense licks inside my ear. Then, as clear as anything, "*Ismene?*"

I don't just know that voice. I know that precise utterance. That moment. I know the shape of it, the rhythm of it. I know the frayed edges my name took on in their hands. I'd forgotten that moment... neglected the memory. God had answered those prayers: let me forget. That was only a temporary reprieve, it seems, and not one that could hold in the quiet, the solitude of this winter nighttime stillness.

The moment was April 1st, 2050. 4:30 P.M.

And it's followed me here.

I don't think.

I just run.

No sooner than the cold punches a cramp into my side, my foot catches a root and I stumble. Instinct kicks in. I tuck the lantern close to my chest, cradling it like a football as I twist to shield it from the impact of our fall. My snowy landing makes little sound beyond the crinkle of the papery roots that tripped me.

No, you tripped on the roots. The roots did not trip you.

This is what I tell myself again and again as I lie there on my back, staring up at the trees and snow. Such a strange perspectival shift the forest takes on from that position. Like the trees are retreating. The snow, too, is retreating. I push myself onto my elbows, but the illusion doesn't break. Still, the snow isn't falling. It rises. Fat, lacy flakes float, up, up, and up—their ascent slow but unrelenting, like ashes buoyed upward by heat. Death and devastation reduced to physical laws. Thermodynamics. Ecology.

Snow collects on the branches above, clumping together in a tangled weave how cotton candy wraps around a stick. It looks like it should be warm to the touch. The way something that's just come from a body ought to be warm to the touch. Something alive. Or, at least, recently alive. Hollow places form within the gossamer tunnels made by snow-turned-silk wrapping itself again and again between and around splayed branches. I can just make out the suggestion of black pits disappearing past the open spaces that gape at the end of every branch, in a hundred misshapen, black maws of swallowed darkness.

The wind picks up. With it comes the rustle of young spring leaves that are not, cannot be there. It makes the branches above me sway, too. Silver-dappled snow webs glisten in the shifting of absent sunlight. As I watch—fascinated, perplexed, terrified—the webs themselves begin to move. No, it's not the webs moving. It's the fog rising between them that's moving. Or is it steam? No. *Smoke.* It's coming off the branches. They're on fire. The forest is on fire. I can't see any fire, but I know they're burning—we're *all* burning—and not because of the smoke.

I can hear them.

They're screaming.

They're screaming because they're trapped in gauzy webs of moth-eaten marrow that's just waiting for the wrong weight, the wrong movement, the wrong touch at the worst possible moment to—

SNAP.

A massive birch tree groans and wines, falling toward me—broken at the base, too heavy to be cowed by the smaller branches and saplings below. I scurry backward, but there was no need. The tree lands, quaking, four paces from the deepest of the footprints I'd left in the snow.

The human mind is a reason-seeking thing—a story-telling thing. That most human of drives corrals my attention into the stretch of black that the tree had once occupied, seeking out a reason... but finding none there. I find nothing but smoke-softened moonlight and the muted freckles of stars. No sooner do I think *how strange it is that the snow's trajectory didn't shift at the motion of such a massive object* that the snow parts itself into a curtain, framing the tree in its absence.

I couldn't see them at first in the white, in the dark. But on that fallen branch, deep within those snow-spun silk tunnels, are stitched dozens of little white moths. *Hundreds* of them. Their wings beat as one. Once, twice, a third time, then they go still. Utterly still. I reach for a window of thinning web, but hesitate once I see little black eyes staring back at me from the other side of the veil.

Hyphantria cunea. Fall webworm.

In perfect sync, hundreds of wings close tight. Moths don't have eyelids. And even though hundreds of tiny black beads still glisten in the moonlight, I can't help but feel they've shut their eyes tight too. Hundreds of nonexistent mouths speak as one.

"Ismene?"

And there it is again. That voice. That precise utterance. That moment.

It's Charlie: just standing there as if a tree hadn't just stood there moments ago, as if a great sundering crack hasn't just torn through the forest.

There they are. My lab assistant, my mentee, my student, my friend. They're here. Standing in the snow. Their skin glows faintly blue just how the snow does. With that, and how their face is softened by a distance greater than the one between us, they look like they're drowning. I reach for them. My hands squeeze and open, forming the shape of their name when I can't speak it again.

But Charlie doesn't reach back. Nor does their mouth move as they whisper through darkness, through impossible snowflakes, through a thousand moths, "Did you report me?"

I shake my head frantically, mouthing, "*No,*" with each motion.

"I trusted you," the night around Charlie says. "Did you get what you wanted?"

"I didn't know what they would do. I didn't *know.*"

"You knew what they would give you."

"I made a mistake. I was *scared* and I made a mistake, I'm *sorry.* I am. But I have a family, Cherise—"

I freeze and stare, mortified. Blue eyes glisten like a fresh wound in the moonlight.

"Oh, God, I am so sorry, I meant—I meant *Charlie*, I swear, you know I've never done that before, you know I haven't, you know that's not who I am"—I rush forward, shoulders hunched, hands up in supplication—"I would never." I take their hands; they're frail—less than cold in mine. "I would *never*, I—"

Words fail me and I kiss their hands instead. They taste sweet: just how forgiveness *should* taste. I kiss them again, and again, and again until my lips only slide clumsily along their skin.

I only stop because I have to. My tongue feels swollen, stuck to every surface of my mouth. I can't open my lips. They've fused shut. I can't open my mouth to gasp my panic, and I'm alone out here again. Charlie is gone. A whimper is all I can manage as I search them out. All I find is trees—trees as far as my lantern can reach. Beyond, where snow used to fall, blue and glittering in the moonlight, is complete darkness

And then here, too is darkness. I can't see. I move toward where I think my lantern should be and stumble. My boot catches on a root and I go down, hard. When I roll to my side, the knife my husband gave me kisses my ankle. *You're here, Ismene,* it says. *You are cold, you are hard, but you are real and you are here.*

Only, the knife isn't cold anymore. Not in my hands.

I make to slice a new smile where I remember my mouth ought to be—where I'm certain my mouth must have been. But it feels so distant now. Rearranged. Cut off by a mad surgeon while I slept, and grafted to some other place entirely. I saw deeper and feel nothing on my lips. I don't feel my lips at all. I keep sawing.

It's only when the knife nicks my earlobe

that I realize just how deeply I've cut. Heat pulses in my throat. A hollow *thump, thump, thump* echoes there too. It's slowing. I can feel my bones now: cold. That coldness spreads, eating away at the core of me. Like cancer. Like an infection. An invasive species. A pestilence. It creeps upward and blots out my vision even as my eyes widen. The blood dripping down my forearms already feels tacky... until it doesn't.

I can't feel my fingers. I rub them together—I *try* to. I don't know if anything's happened. I don't know anything—can't see anything. All I hear is a little sound, tremulous and repetitive. Drip? Tap? Flutter? Dripping makes sense.

Drip, drip, drip. Dripping, yes. Because with every drip, I sink a little deeper into the cold.

Snow stings the weak spots on my teeth. Did I fall? Am I lying down now? The drips have gone. Now, it's only *tap... tap... tap.*

Yes? Hello?

Is someone there?

Who is it?

Have you seen my lantern?

I think I understand now. I think I know what that *tap, tap, tapping* is.

It's the moth's wings beating against the lantern's insides, searching out a wound from which to escape.

1-789-0909-1111: Explain yourself.

1-789-0909-6969: I'm a Libra. The fuck is this, a Leo?

1-789-0909-1111: This is the scholar whose paper you commented on through a closing elevator door.

1-789-0909-1111: Rather invectively, I might add. You said more in twenty seconds than I've heard you say for months. Explain yourself.

1-789-0909-6969: Oh.

1-789-0909-6969: Howdy, Professor Angelo?

1-789-0909-1111: You are new to this Ph.D. program, so perhaps you didn't realize that decimating a fellow scholar's core argument then dramatically flouncing before giving said scholar a chance for rebuttal is considered bad form.

1-789-0909-1111: Don't apologize, we've already established you find apologies counterproductive. Explain.

1-789-0909-6969: I was just suggesting that sometimes it feels like we're all treating apologizing like it's a complete act in itself and not an obligation. Conflating contrition and atonement.

1-789-0909-1111: How so?

1-789-0909-6969: Have you read The Metamorphoses?

1-789-0909-1111: Of course.

1-789-0909-1111: Not lately.

1-789-0909-6969: No? There's no annual Arbor Day tradition of rereading Ovid in Mercia? Surely at Oxford?!

1-789-0909-1111: Cute. What about the Metamorphoses?

1-789-0909-6969: Apollo slays his boy-toy with a discus. By accident. But he killed him.

1-789-0909-1111: Hyacinthus.

1-789-0909-6969: Apollo is cradling his dying lover and weeping over his wounds, right? And he says something like "This wound is my doing," but then immediately after is all, "But how can I be responsible when I was just playing a game?" Like, I didn't intend to kill him, I'm just following the rules of the game. I didn't write the rules so nobody can be mad at me.

1-789-0909-1111: Okay... your point being?

1-789-0909-6969: My point is Apollo's point was so BEYOND the point. It served zero purpose.

1-789-0909-1111: Because he hadn't accepted responsibility?

1-789-0909-6969: Because he made it about responsibility at all. Even if he'd come to the conclusion that he was responsible, he'd still be missing the point.

1-789-0909-1111: And what is the point Apollo and I are missing?

1-789-0909-6969: That it doesn't fucking matter. You're a god. Just heal him and bring him back to life! But no, he's too late because he was too busy mourning to actually fix anything.

1-789-0909-1111: And you see a parallel to this in the SMEE?

1-789-0909-6969: In the reaction to the SMEE, yeah.

1-789-0909-1111: What do YOU propose?

1-789-0909-6969: We need to move the conversation past the "weeping over our dead boyfriend" stage. We need to just... idk all accept responsibility. One big act of radical responsibility. We're all responsible.

1-789-0909-1111: If we're all responsible, no one is

responsible.

1-789-0909-6969: Only if you're thinking in the sense Apollo is—that responsibility is something about the past. I'm talking about being responsible FOR something the way a shepherd is responsible for their flock. Not the way that shepherd is responsible for manslaughter via frisbee.

1-789-0909-1111: You should write this down.

1-789-0909-6969: Should I use a fountain pen?

1-789-0909-1111: You should. It may help you curb your excess language.

1-789-0909-6969: That paper comment sure touched a nerve, huh

1-789-0909-1111: No.

1-789-0909-1111: Handwriting won't only improve your style. There is an accessibility to pens lacked by typing.

1-789-0909-6969: I find typing perfectly accessible. Do you have any idea how expensive ink is these days?

1-789-0909-1111: Wrong accessibility. We used to FEEL what we were writing.

1-789-0909-6969: We also used to waste gallons of

potable water every day flushing toilets, and carpet bomb insects to grow corn so we could throw it away.

1-789-0909-1111: Is this newfound social ease attributable to alcohol?

1-789-0909-6969: Maybe.

1-789-0909-1111: If that was your drunk critique, I'm not certain my ego could handle you sober.

1-789-0909-6969: you're self aware though and that's important.

1-789-0909-1111: You don't strike me as the party Ph.D. type.

1-789-0909-6969: I'm not. Just... stupid personal stuff.

1-789-0909-1111: Explain.

1-789-0909-6969: First Valentine's Day since my partner left me is all. You know how it is.

1-789-0909-1111: No. I've never been left.

1-789-0909-6969: False.

1-789-0909-1111: ?

1-789-0909-6969: You got left this afternoon, via elevator. You probably just forgot because it's already been three hours.

1-789-0909-1111: Is there anything you won't challenge me on?

1-789-0909-6969: Probably not, no.

1-789-0909-1111: Good.

1-789-0909-6969: Is it REALLY good though?

1-789-0909-1111: I changed my mind. You're not cute.

1-789-0909-6969: :C

1-789-0909-1111: Go to bed. I expect you in my office first thing tomorrow morning.

1-789-0909-6969: Yes sir.

Part II: *Allomone*

Twelve graduate students sit around a large ovular conference table. It dominates the space. In the semi-darkness, the same indigo, lavender, and green light dapples all twelve faces. The source is the techboard-projected image hovering between them: the last known photograph of the last known wild hyacinth. It demands their attention and their averted gazes all at once, like a portrait at a wake—reminding the mourners just whom they're mourning.

I watch them all from my place in the corner, thumbs casually hooked in the pockets of my black jeans. "Observe the cupped shape of the petals... the fluted edges... the inviting curl of the lip.... beckoning stamens. Positively seductive. Even for us. And yet, arguably, not *for* us. Why not? Or, is it simply a matter of why *not yet*?"

Nathane shakes her head, purple-painted mouth twisted. "Doubtful," she says. "You can't possibly expect a plant that's spent centuries—millennia, in most cases—coevolving with a particular pollinator to just be able to change their stripes."

Rainer's leaning forward: eager to jump in, waiting for a lull in the back-and-forth tide of conversation. His desperation to engage, be heard, makes his shirt ruck up. A stretch of skin on his lower back (the precise shade I take my coffee: with a hearty splash of milk), teases me. I can practically feel the tickle of fine hair on my palm. I flex my hand and tip another ladle-full of chum into the waters. "Change what, precisely?"

"No, wait, that's right," Isis says. A nontraditional student: older than her fellow grad students by twenty years. She taps one finger on the table, beating out the rhythm of her thoughts. It is deeply obnoxious. "It's not as if they'd have to switch up their genetic presentation. The same floral structure they used to attract their insect pollinators is also attractive to human pollinators."

"But there's no mechanism for feedback," Nathane persists. She's incredibly invested—mostly in being correct... or, in being perceived as being correct. If that fire could be applied to botany, she'd be a formidable force. But as she said: you can't just expect a being to change their stripes. "Coevolution isn't just a matter of ending up with a physical form that can attract a pollinator. It's a product of communication. Plants speak and listen to their environments. Humans can't communicate with plants the way a caterpillar or wasp can. We just can't!"

I click my tongue. "Certainly not with that

attitude, no."

Rainer sees his opening in the intermission formed by quiet laughter. "Rye domesticated itself."

I give him an approving smile: subtle, but he's keen enough to recognize it. His responding smile is far, far less subtle. "Explain," I say. Every student (even Nathane) has straightened to attention, preparing to take notes. They recognize that I've heard what I've been waiting to hear. One of them has finally managed to say something worth writing down. Isis' fingers are poised over her iWrite. Most, however—Rainer included—have adopted their professor's peculiar habit of writing by hand, with ink. Heron has gone so far as to procure himself a fountain pen—steel and plastic. Not one I myself would use, but it's endearing in its own way. A *teensy* bit pathetic, but mostly endearing. Flattering, certainly.

I fold my arms across my chest, prepared to listen. Had I not been perfectly aware of the effect my arms straining against black short-sleeve t-shirt would have on Rainer, I would be now. "Rainer?" I prod gently.

Rainer's skin flushes, but only at the very base of his throat, lighting up his delicate clavicle like a crown. The scope is barely visible, but I know it stretches past his collar. His throat must be where it starts. That won't be where it finishes. His nipples, maybe. Navel, even. None of these thoughts show on my face; only a vague sort of patient impatience. "Sorry," he says. "Rye domesticated itself. It was growing in wheat fields, and the farmers were constantly pulling it up and tossing it away. So it changed to become more desirable to humans, and now it's something we intentionally grow. Steward."

"That's not the whole story, though," Nathane points out. "Rye *imitated* wheat. It wasn't trying to become more desirable to us, it was trying to imitate its neighbors that *weren't* getting ripped out of the ground each morning."

"We can't say what the plant meant to do or if it meant to do anything at all," Heron says. His voice is steadfast as he paraphrases a passage from my most recent book, using it as a handrail. "We only know the result: We protect it."

Isis snorts. "We *eat* it."

Rainer dives back in. "Yes, but we also facilitate its reproduction on a scale it never could have achieved without us. To a plant, *reproduction* is success, *not* avoiding being eaten."

Nathane opens her mouth, doubtlessly to point out that we can no more ascribe notions of success to plants than we can infer their intentions, but she's cut off by Heron.

"And since we help the plant reproduce," Heron says, "it keeps growing how we want it to."

An oversimplification.

The haptic feedback of Isis' typing fingers on her iWrite is deeply agitating. The technological equivalent of someone chewing a caramel, mouth open. I close my eyes and press a finger to my temple. "So that begs the question then: What, if anything, was pollinating rye before its self-domestication?" My eyes open up to a dozen faces, expecting an answer. I don't give them one. "If you can answer that question, you can answer most in this seminar. Be prepared to discuss next class. Until next week." As the students begin filtering out, I snap my fingers and point. "And be ready to discuss your final paper topics." Grimaces meet me. "The more easily you can discuss and *defend* your ideas out loud with your peers, the clearer your writing will be, and the more compelling your argument will be."

Every face bears a trace of determination. They know I'm right. Most of the students wish to succeed to impress me, earn my regard. Some wish to succeed out of some warped notion of spite. A prejudice inherited from their own preferred idols in the department—either Professor Ross, Washington, or Ziarek, no doubt. Blind enmity.

Asinine. Completely fucking asinine.

Just imagine how much science could have accomplished without all this pissy academic in-fighting. For one thing, they'd probably have proper flower specimens to examine. Not just their ghosts.

Rainer's lingering between the table and the doorway the rest of his peers have just departed through. Big, brown eyes are fixed on the slowly rotating hyacinth even as he speaks to me—as the rest of his body is oriented so firmly toward nothing but me. "I was just hoping we could discuss my final paper topic?" he asks. As the flower keeps spinning, the hazy colors projected upon his face shift, painting his lips in darker and lighter petal shades.

"Certainly." I shut down the projection, robbing Rainer's face of its Monet wash of indigos and greens.

Rainer's eyes finally move to mine then. "Maybe tonight?" he offers, words charged with hope. The intent is apparent (and flattering), but wholly inappropriate. And not only because of the titanium ring catching reflected hyacinth petals on my right hand. It's that moment I realize that the department chair has been looming in the hallway outside the door for fuck-knows how long. Nguyen's round face is a carved, expressionless pumpkin, and its hollow eyes are fixed on me. Not so much as an eyebrow twitches when he notices I've noticed him.

"No," I tell Rainer, tone kind but firm. "My regular office hours are always available to you. Feel free to make an appointment."

Rainer nods, a weak smile at one corner of his mouth. "Okay, I'll email you."

"Do that." I lean against the conference table. "Professor Nguyen," I say, "to what do I owe the honor?"

"*Hyacinthus orientalis*," Nguyen says, giving me a look like a seal expecting a fish or something. "The wild type, I believe."

"Good eye." My smile is paper-thin, but I know it's passable enough. Nguyen isn't harmless because he is an idiot. If he can't find an organic opening to inform—rather, remind you that he attended Cambridge, he will perform the information to the best of his ability. He's gearing up for a performance now: all but bouncing on his feet already. He expects me, being half English, to be particularly enamored by this biographical bit of detritus.

I am not.

"Did you know," Nguyen begins, "that the flower identified by Homer was almost certainly *not* what we've come to identify as *Hyacinthus,* but rather a variety of *Scilla*?"

I did. "I did not, no," I say with a spark of interest.

True to form, Nguyen is positively *aglow.* "Indeed! And do you know the fabled origin of this flower?"

I do. Quite well. "Something to do with Hermes, yes?"

"Apollo!"

"Ah. My mistake."

"Tragedy is not new to the Olympics, I'm afraid."

"Yes, I heard about that. Awful stuff." I blow out a breath and ask, "Was there something I can do for you, Professor?"

Nguyen's moment of grimacing hesitation doesn't inspire confidence. "There was... there was, yes." The man's attention drifts over my shoulder, to the wall of windows.

"Would your office be—"

"Yes," the old man says, eyes still fixed on

whatever he found beyond the glass. Despite that, he does not walk. Does not move. Not even his eyes. "We've had an interesting funding offer from a private interest. Unfortunately, the timeline is rather compressed."

Typical. "Silicon Valley?"

"Florida. Field research in the Western Expanse, visa access granted to two scholars. Your name was given special mention as 'nonnegotiable.'"

I don't know what to say to that. The Free Republic of Florida is hard enough to get entry into, let alone the Western Expanse. That wilderness is an untapped hoard of scientific advancement, and the FRF has cordoned it off with all the jealousy of an insecure man with a beautiful lover. I am far from the only ecologist convinced there are solutions hidden behind those barricades—and *only* behind those barricades. We've been preparing for the day the FRF sees sense and grants us access for years.

Or for the day the rest of the continent sees sense and *forces* the issue.

I look to the window in the vague hope I might glean whatever's captured the chair's interest. All I see is empty sky and bare branches. "What are they looking for?" I ask.

"They won't tell you until you get there. But, as it's *you* they've requested in particular, we can guess."

Sabbatical had been 'suggested' to me already. As taking it would be as good as conceding defeat—and culpability—I've flatly denied that suggestion. "And if I refuse?"

Nguyen blinks, startled. That possibility had not occurred to him. "You'd be a fool."

"Being a fool is hardly a consequence."

"You're a clever man, Leon. You're well aware of the consequences."

My voice goes quiet, brittle. "I was the only one here *fighting for* Shiloh's funding! And you know damned well they haven't any evidence." Even as I say it, we both know the truth. They don't need it.

"You wish to protect your career?" Nguyen asks. "Then leave. And while you are gone, do something great. Be *undeniable*."

The fact that I always have been undeniable is likely why I'm still here. But with each whisper of innuendo in the hallway after department meetings, the bar for just how great a scholar needs to be creeps ever higher. If the FRF is swallowing its pride down deep enough to seek outside help—from Californians, no less—it must be big.

Undeniable.

"Very well. Tell me more."

The northerly route through the Western Expanse is the least forgiving. Naturally, it's the only one the FRF will make available to non-nationals. It was only through the combined scholastic merit of myself (the authority in my own peculiar subfield), and Val Rowan (the authority in hers), that we were considered for entry permission at all. By which I mean we (evidently) inspired a private donor with government connections to petition for our being granted entry. This may well be the first time in CNU history that any scholar has received such a generous grant without needing to hire multiple R.A.s to perfect their application package, let alone not *apply at all.*

Generous, yes. But a swamp is still a swamp. Even in February, even for a forty-eight-year-old man as physically fit as myself, even completely devoid of disease-carrying insects, a swamp is still a swamp. Trudging through knee-high bog soup with nothing but rotting tree carcasses to steady our balance burns a lot of calories and even more daylight, however robust you are.

Ahead of me, Val (who only just returned from an expedition to her home country of Australia) struggles to keep her balance with the massive pack of supplies on her back. The shaved half of her head is sun-chapped and glistening with sweat where it isn't caked with dirt. If my fingernails are any indication, I don't look much better.

As the temperature drops, the sweat soaked into my shirt makes itself known. No longer at my body temperature, the moisture prickles and chaps against my skin—invasive. I hadn't thought to pack wool base layers, what with it being *Florida.* Foolish.

It's been a hot minute since I've led an expedition of grad students up through the city-high forests of the Pacific Northwest, or down the Sierra Nevadas' spine. Any blistered heels or muggy stretches of marshland were always offset by purple mountains majesty and the thrill of discovery. Both were made far keener thanks to the eyes of young scholars, still brimming with curiosity. All too young to be jaded, knowing nothing but possibility and hope for the future, looking to me with something akin to awe. Not that I ever accepted awe. I've always gone out of my way to make sure *my* grad students knew every one of their professors is just another person. And we are all *scholars* in our own right. Equals.

If my old advisor could see me at the lectern, he'd spin so fast in his tweed-lined casket he'd make *sparks*. By my second semester teaching, I'd ditched the blazers he'd insisted were as essential to the field of biology as a working knowledge of Latin and Greek, and taken up an unofficial uniform of black jeans and black t-shirts. How are students meant to truly engage in—really get *invested* in—scholarship if they can't see themselves as part of the intellectual community? Not just as a second-class secretary taking notes after the fact, but a valuable conversant? *Somebodies* with *something* to say?

Again and again I hear my colleagues (not just in Botany or ecology, but any discipline) lamenting the lack of active participation in their classrooms. If they could drop the ego and post-Ph. D. trauma long enough to step down from the podium and get to their students' levels—low enough to see them as people and not *registrants*—they wouldn't have to bitch about it in Starbucks. If I thought they would *hear* me, I'd tell them I don't only speak to my students like they can understand me. I *listen* to them like they have something worth saying. And when I lead them on expeditions, I eat the same throat-clogging dehydrated food, sip at a snail's pace from the same filtration tubes that never go unclogged for more than twenty seconds, bathe in the same slimy-rock lined, leech-filled streams. I sleep fitfully in the same tents, and roll around on the same muddy ground as them.

For me, two years is a long time to be out of the field. That's not why every step on this brittle loam we're treading over now is a struggle, though. Florida is an unforgiving climate. This section of the continent doesn't know what to do with itself weather-wise, but it still can't manage meteorological aberrance in any mode other than *unforgiving*.

The Western Expanse, true to name, expands from northern Florida all the way to what was once eastern Louisiana. Its weather patterns have become so capricious, even Californian scientists struggle to predict them. This month's freezing temperatures weren't exactly *anticipated*. Otherwise, I'd have packed appropriately. *Miserable*. The air is heavy here. Cold and wet. Like breathing in pneumonia. I've been ignoring just how hard it is to take a full breath for hours now. My shins won't be ignored so easily; they're screaming for a break like a cranky toddler on a road trip, but we can't stop. Waypoint Four is still miles off, and navigating in a dead zone—relying on nothing but questionable compasses and even more questionable paper maps—is hard enough without adding darkness to the mix. It would be pretty fucking typical for Floridian jackboots to give the faggot and the dyke faulty equipment.

Val shoots a glance over her shoulder, says nothing. She only continues onward, doubtlessly thinking what I am: until we've set up camp, we can't afford the darkness.

I force my heart rate to slow by drawing air deep from my diaphragm.

The flesh is weak, but my mind is among the strongest in the field.

I can handle one little fucking Florida *cold snap*.

Not much distinguishes Waypoint Four from the rest of the jungle. Six orange peltate markers labeled with FRF's national sigil and a peeling **IV** denote the perimeter. One dangling from a rusted nail driven into the heart of a pine heralds a half-buried storage crate filled (in theory) with emergency supplies, its white plastic jaundiced by the sun. There's plenty enough space for two tents and a shared workstation. Val wordlessly shrugs off her massive pack and pitches her tent in the corner farthest from the strip of standing water which borders one edge of the area. We've got an hour of twilight left, max. I follow suit, unpacking my tent by the mossy ground near the stray scrap of marsh. It's already cold and only going to get colder at night. Val, though, is shrugging out of her fleece and plucking at her shirt's chest.

Even knowing what I know of our planet's prognosis, I can't help but be grateful for the lack of insects while we work. Steam comes off in plumes from nearby the water which is far warmer than the air. It inches closer and reaches for our feet like spectral hands, threatening us with the twitch-in-the-ear feeling that just *imagining* a buzzing swarm brings. Epigenetic aversion has yet to adjust to the year 2061. Forgetting a hundred plagues born by millions of insects is no mean feat for DNA. After the cloning projects take off and the collective trauma of this lonely, silent planet passes into memory, how many generations will it take before our descendants can shed their own timid, scarred genes? How long before they stop reflexively recoiling in silence?

I haven't pitched a tent in some time, but it goes up with little fuss. My temporary, powder-blue nylon home is hardly grand, but it's space aplenty when you're sleeping alone. Behind me, I hear Val's tent zip shut. She's hardly spoken a word to me these past few days, but that's hardly unusual for her. If I'm a social butterfly, she's a crotchety mantis. But she's a good scientist with the respect of her students—and I'd have heard otherwise if she didn't. Students confide in me. They know they can trust I won't judge them for being intimidated by their professors or for feeling lost in a swamp of readings and exams and lab work. Or, they *did* confide in me. Confiding in one's teacher about one's *other* teacher is somewhat precarious when my office door (which occupies a wing shared by said other teachers' office doors) must remain open during office hours. Yet one more asinine policy ostensibly meant to protect students that, in reality, only makes them more vulnerable to those with the power to harm them.

Impropriety is a serious charge for what's essentially *pearl clutching* from colleagues too stubborn to recognize themselves as the source of the problem plaguing every department: dwindling enrollment. Try telling that to the chair. *Dead Poets' Society* is seventy years old: a classic that's definitely permeated the collective cultural consciousness— among the educated, certainly. Surely scapegoating the one teacher students can actually relate to is a bit *old hat*.

Tragedies happen. I wish to God *that* tragedy hadn't. But doctoral programs are tough, and students don't get the financial or mental health support they need to flourish. Is it any wonder a student stripped of his T.A.ship would kill himself? Tragic. Truly. But the real tragedy is the fact that the University saw its chance to avoid blaming the institution making it millions in profits every year:

by blaming the kid's advisor instead.

Fuck, it's nearly been *two years* since we lost Shiloh. And I still can't enter a departmental event without feeling like a leper. Not that any of them would ever say jack. If their sneers and hinted allegations ever rise above the shadows, every administrator getting rich off the research of scholars—and making four times their salaries—will hear exactly what I think of them, of what higher education's become, and where they can stick their *allegations*.

Fuck it. They may hear it anyway. Washington, Ross, and Ziarek don't even try to be subtle. They shield their chosen acolyte students from me like hissing chickens, burdened with chicks too stupid to cross the street on their own. Those students don't even know why they're offended by my persisting existence. They've just *heard things*. Behavioral conditioning amplified by malicious influence. You can pick them out a mile off. They're impossible to miss at conferences and colloquia. I know what those plastic smiles in the hallway mean: *I don't need to hear the evidence. I don't need to hear your side of the story. I don't even need to hear what the ostensible crime was. I've judged you already, and that judgment is guilty.*

Several meters beyond the orange marks, Val is examining a dead snag. She catches my eye and doesn't smile, plastically or otherwise. So far as I can tell, she doesn't know how. If that woman agrees with her more histrionic colleagues, she never hints at it. She may not even be aware of the overblown scandal's existence. The only thing that offends her more than departmental drama is drone rot in cash crops. No one else had even known that she has a wife and child until the university switched health insurance providers. Processing a request for leave was how they'd learned of said child's death. Personal details shared via bureaucracy, and bureaucracy alone.

Val is ever a pragmatist and, quite probably, my favorite colleague.

She shoots me a look: not concerned, not offended, not bothered with much at all. If anything, she's just checking I've not wandered off into that little patch of swamp and drowned. Purely for food-rationing purposes. A breath of fresh pre-twenty-first-century air. I respect the fuck out of Dr. Val Rowan... even if she does research plant "intelligence."

What is she staring at?

"Val?" I ask, but my throat's crackly from lack of use. I clear it and try again. "Val?"

Val doesn't acknowledge me. She just keeps staring off into the quickly darkening forest, arms tight at her sides.

"Val."

She does turn this time, her face its typical neutral mask.

I ask, "Did you see something?"

Her eyes drift. "No," she says, her deep voice quiet. "Just thinking."

I don't bother asking what about. "We should get to bed if we're going to make the best of what daylight we have tomorrow."

She agrees with a nod then shoots me another in silent *goodnight.*

"Good night," I say and slip into my own tent. Just before I've finished zipping the flap shut, I can see that Val has not done the same. Her back is turned to me, but I'm certain she's still at the perimeter, staring into the darkness. Who knows? Maybe the darkness is staring back.

That would explain why she felt the need to give it that shy, little wave.

There's little overlap in our paths for now. Val is working her way north, taking soil samples and obsessively documenting surrounding conditions. I'm headed south to observe any changes in native epiphytes since Bateman's 2034 study. They've been evolving at a remarkable rate these past few decades. The Christo-fascists of our host country have taken this as proof that evolution is pure bunk. Ergo, their twisted little minds reason, *intelligent design* is the only "logical" explanation. Only dramatic recreations of these fairytale arguments over wine keep the rest of the scientific community from breaking down completely. It's very much a "laugh to keep from crying" situation. But, if some poor, wayward Floridian scientific refugee comes to my office, asking me to pretty-please explain the devil's anus that is rudimentary *evo-fucking-lution*, I'll oblige. *Giddily.*

It takes three weeks before I can even find one of the four orchid species I've designated for study. *Dendrophylax lindenii* was a ghost before the SMEE. Its rarity makes the name appropriate, but little else. In pre-2030 photographs, the flowers looked more like frogs than ghosts. Now, of course, the flowers are next to nonexistent: little more than a tangle of photosynthetic roots, its leaves and flowers alike devolved to small, scale-like pseudobuds on its labyrinthine body. Were I a betting man, this is not the orchid I'd have predicted finding first. It's always been finicky, reclusive. It favors growing on flowering trees which are themselves dependent upon pollinators, but now reliant entirely on wind—at least here, where drones can't reach without breaking down just yards past the border.

Whole place is a dead zone.

And yet, here is a pond-apple tree. Fruitless, yes, but the waxy almond leaves give it away. A green just the right shade for the ghost orchid to conceal itself. These flowers can try to hide what they really are, the truth of them, but I've been doing this for decades. I could spot a tangle of epiphyte roots just about anywhere. It's sheer intuition at this point.

I mark the spot, document every bit of minutia (by hand, of course) before moving on.

On the way back to camp, the telltale coil of epiphytic roots stops me. This cluster of papery ribbons at the base of a pine tree might have blended in perfectly, if not for the unusual formation: not many branching from a single point as in a tree or weed, but many descending from a horizontal line of many points.

Crack.

I nearly gasp. On the forest floor, blended perfectly amidst a coil those rust-brown roots, is a dead animal. So perfectly blended, in fact, I have to crouch low to convince myself that I'm really seeing what I think I'm seeing. It's a fox or coyote. Impossible to tell at this point—at least, to a *botanist.* It's rotting, though one could hardly tell from the smell... or lack thereof. It's as if it's been mummified. But in a forest edging on subtropical? Unlikely. Roots surround it, coiling about it in the very shape that animal curled up and died in. Rather like a napping cat in a patch of sun. It might even look serene in other circumstances, if the jawbone hadn't been eaten away to expose missing, broken teeth and pearly bone... if not for the misshapen hole where a tongue should be.

What remains of the pitiful thing's teeth are embedded in a thick vine—probably so desperate for food after the die-off of birds and rodents, it tried to eat the forest itself. And that's where it died. Frozen forever in a moment of starved desperation. It's the sort of thing one sees in tar pits: casts of drowning saber-toothed tigers, its claws forever welded inside its fellow drowning traveler.

The sun's yet to set, but I pull out my torch to see the odd formation better before reaching out to touch a desiccated shoulder—

"Fucking hell."

I rapidly retract my hand at the unsavory *crinkle* this canid's flesh makes at the barest touch. Using a nearby stick this time, I push back some mottled, gray-brown fur. Just as surely as its fangs had embedded itself in this root, the roots have wormed their way into its ribs. Stranger yet, the animal's own flesh seems to have taken on the texture of those roots. How odd. Plenty of plant species possess the ability to mimic their neighbors: plant or animal. But the reverse simply makes no sense. What would be the evolutionary advantage in a posthumous transformation? Some manner of epigenetic spite playing out on the wild stage? More likely a coincidence. An undeniably *unsettling* coincidence, but a coincidence all the same.

Perhaps it's mycelium? It would make perfect sense for a fungus to work its way through a corpse. Rotting meat isn't much good to a plant, but it is perfectly bioavailable to a fungus. No, the roots aren't thin enough. The color's wrong, too. They're a deep reddish brown, not white or gray. Too large, not nearly tangled enough. That doesn't exclude the possibility that a fungus—perhaps a microscopic species—has attached itself to this plant. Come to think of it, I don't think I've seen any mushrooms since we've arrived. A quick torchlight survey up and down the tree reveals no source of these roots. No leaves, no bulbs, no pseudobuds to speak of.

I'm losing light. Time to mark the spot and move on. It's fully dark by the time I make it back to Waypoint Four. Val's tent is a red lantern beyond the trees. Inside, her hunched silhouette is doubtlessly doing what I'm now settling in to do: translate field notes from chicken scratch to something legible. Using paper is necessitated by circumstance for her, but not me. I favor handwritten notes. Pure cotton is my preferred medium. It takes a skilled, confident hand to avoid making a mess of irreplaceable data. The right pen for the job is just as crucial as the hand holding it, and the nib must be gold.

I realize I'm something of an oddity, misplaced in time. Fountain pens were anachronous even during my grandparents' day. As eccentric as my habit of handwriting makes me in the academe, however, it does make me well suited to operating in dead zones like this.

My hand stays loose, letting the pen's weight dictate the pressure, control the flow. I sketch out the rough shape of the Western Expanse: something like a bursting bouquet of paper flowers, stems bundled at the Florida archipelago and spilling its bounty into what used to be Louisiana, Alabama, George, Tennessee, and most of the Carolinas. Then, I move on to the ghost orchid, making long, elegant sweeps for its shy, vine-like rhizome. I'm careful, intentional with my pen strokes—responsive to the surface beneath my hand.

When done right, there is something undeniably erotic about penmanship. Botany, too, should be somewhat erotic. For much of the history of science, nature was feminized. *She.* Mother Nature. Her primitive wild. Something to be tamed. Dissected. Dominated. We must conquer *her.* Such metaphors have (happily) been scrubbed from the discourse. But still... there is *something* of value there that we've lost. We could all stand to regain a sense of the erotic in natural philosophy.

Taking the time and care to take notes by hand is just one way of paying homage to that commitment. The firm press of the hand on paper, the soft give of gold against pulp. The repetitive strokes, broken up by moments of hovering hesitation whilst waiting for the object of study to whisper what it all means—what it *needs.* No wonder I've been accused of extravagant poeticism at so many conferences. The fact that I always have both the data and the analytical rigor to back it up is what has made me who I am today. When people see *Dr. Leon Angelo, CNU* on a program, they take note. They attend (if only for the animated Q&A session afterward).

My huffed laugh forms a cloud in front of me. When was the last time I could see my breath like that...? *Vancouver?* Yes: my last expedition. Fuck me, has it already been two years? When figuring the years by passive-aggressive looks on campus, it seems a decade has passed. But when counting backward from him, it's only moments.

Shiloh… always struggling to get the I.T. department and campus security to believe he was a doctoral candidate and T.A., not a lost undergrad. No wonder: that soft face made him look more like a teenager than the late-twenty-something he was. Who could resent such a face? Such a body? How gracefully it moved, even when scrambling up a rock face, harness digging into his pants and binding his ass just tightly enough to suggest the shape of the rest of him—the crease that kept going.

How shy he was in the tent. How demure.

The sounds he'd make.

That's the Shiloh I still see, in the quiet moments. I didn't go to the funeral, though as his advisor, I was invited— expected, even. I have no regrets. Perhaps that's selfish of me. But the only version of Shiloh's face *I* remember is the smooth, youthful, blushing one. Curling brown hair—soft, not matted with congealed blood. Eyes bright and brown, not dull and sunken. And a body with that perfect blend of muscle and softness that made him look less like a modern-day grad student and far more like the beloved of some Greek god. Shiloh was like me: born into the wrong age. One without any gods left to chase him. A tragic waste.

That boy would have made *such* a constellation.

My chin hitting my chest snaps me awake.

Something's cold. Wet. My hand's smeared ink across my last diagram. I mouth a curse which gets far more creative once I clock that my fountain pen has been leeching ink into my pillow via capillary action. Sleeping bag, too. "Oh, fuck me with an epiphyte!"

"—ask me again and I'll do it."

I freeze, ink-bruised hand hovering stupidly beside me. "Val?"

No answer. Just the wind shaking bare branches, rustling nylon. I grab my little flashlight and unzip the tent with one hand while clumsily slipping on my shoes with the other. The only light around is the blue-tinted glow from my own tent. I switch off my lantern to see the rest of the world better. My torch's circle of gold light bounces along the forest floor, skipping over moss, roots, and rocks before hitting red. I don't know what time it is. Late.

Val's tent is dark, but not silent. Subdued sounds filter out, more like tongue-clicking and chewing than speech—like somebody gnawing, toothless on a bone. It's only when her voice rises that words come through:

"—know you did, baby."

I don't need to check my own comm or geo-locator to know that both are only useful as paperweights out here. She's sleep talking. Must be. Even in this uncanny wild, it would take far longer than a handful of weeks for a scholar like Val Rowan to lose her mind.

More mouth-smacking sounds. The *pit-pat* of

locking and unlocking lips. Shifting nylon. She's probably rolling around (or, trying to) in her sleeping bag. Sleep talking it is, then. Best to give her privacy.

Between the frozen crunch of my footsteps, a few more words follow me back to my tent. *"Sweet baby, I will never, ever let you go again."*

Shuddering leaves tag along after the words, heralding an incoming breeze. It's hot when it comes. A stream of shockingly warm air washes over me, forcing me to sway backward—then into it. It's as if some great beast laid down in between the trees and sighed, all its considerable body heat warming the forest twenty degrees, making a microclimate with its mouth.

Heat licks up my throat. The wind groans. I snap my mouth shut once I realize that groan was mine. *Am I actually sweating right now?* It's *freezing*. It *was* freezing. Now, my thermal layers feel suffocating. Tight. I tug at my collar in a futile attempt to stretch out the fleece that had been so necessary for my comfort just moments ago. I bite the middle finger of my glove and tug it off, tossing it to the ground. It's when I think to remove the other that I realize my other hand has already started sliding down my abdomen in teasing touches—entirely of its own accord. Maybe my dreams were far more immersive for my body than my mind recalls. Said mind recognizes the importance of maximizing the little time we have left by getting a solid night's rest.

But my fingers are flexing at the memory of how soft Shiloh's hair had felt gripped between them. How tight he was.

However strong my mind may be, the flesh is still weak.

For fuck's sake, am I a fucking teenager? However hard I will my body to calm down, to obey me, my libido only takes this as a challenge. Need pulses in my balls, plucking at the core of me: *thrum, thrum, thrum.*

If the hitch in my breath with every drag of fabric over my steadily hardening dick is any indication, this won't take long. Nylon isn't exactly soundproof, though, and the sound of what my fist is about to be doing is pretty un-fucking-mistakable. The wind is picking up, but I can't count on the wet sounds of pumping not to filter through Val's tent in the stiller moments. Last thing my reputation needs is a second accusation of impropriety: *Famed botany researcher can't contain his rampant horniness long enough to jerk off out of earshot of female colleague.*

Fuck it.

I take my flashlight and search out a discreet corner of wilderness. It isn't hard. This whole forest is discreet. All my flashlight reveals is hundreds of bare trees, none distinguishable from their neighbors' shadows. A monotonous pattern of bars repeats itself into infinite dark. I stumble over a patch of gravel and groan at the shift of fabric at my crotch. It's warm here. So fucking *warm*. I don't slow my awkward march for a moment as I strip my last two top layers, leaving behind an incriminating trail of fabric.

That last trip in the Sierra Nevadas feels so close. *Shiloh* feels so close. It's as if my mind's made some sort of bargain—trading dream for sensual reality. The memories seem so much realer, so much *thicker* than the forest around me. It must be the relative sensory deprivation of this blank wilderness.

Another pulse of hot air against my throat and chest pushes me back—a thick pine catches me. The bite of bark against my back just makes my dick twitch. I let my knees bend, dragging down, down. This exquisite pain is fingernails raking down my back. I land between two massive, fluted tree roots. I feel out the round shape of them, molding my hands to cup them better. The stiff, flaking texture of pine gives way to something soft. Something warm. Something with give. I close my eyes, and my world lights up. My thumbs press harder, and the roots part at my touch, displaying the lover who'd been waiting for me there this whole time.

Shiloh's blushing thighs open up to me—his lover, his teacher—and reveal the sweet truth of him. His pussy's dripping for me already: wet and warm and wanting. He reaches a hand down to his hole and smears that slickness up, circling the nascent dick coaxed from a woman's body by bottled testosterone. Making the cute little red thing glisten. It twitches, shy in my mouth when I suck on it.

He smells sweet... innocuous. Like a woman.

He tastes like one, too.

Shiloh just lies there and lets me do whatever I want to him. Not because I am the master of my imagination. Because even in my most objective of memories, my boy was never anything shy of supplicant beneath my hands... my mouth. He bites back plaintive little sounds each time I brush my lips over his poor excuse for stubble, the half-suggestion of an Adam's apple.

He covers that perfect, blushing boy's face with his hands while I fuck the truth out of him. I don't stop until his deep grunts become feeble, whining lilts that might have been mistaken for singing if he weren't getting railed by his advisor in the dirt.

My whole being coils up on itself and pulls taut. My hand pumps faster as my mind's eye breeds Shiloh the way only *boys like him* can be bred. With consequences. *Real* consequences. There's power there in knowing just how deeply, how irrevocably I can change his life, his body, his being—just by pinning him to the ground and fucking him how a body like that was made to be fucked. I come inside that pussy, and I don't stop fucking my cum into him until my legs go numb.

That thought finishes me off. I finish with a groan so quiet, my load makes more sound when it spatters the roots below. It takes me half a minute for my thighs to feel like they can support my weight again. Val could come this way, looking for evidence of whatever fungus it is she's obsessed with these days. Hate for her to take a sample thinking it's some sort of slime mold. Better cover it up with some dirt and leaves or something. I get my trousers back on, tuck myself up and flick on my flashlight—

There *is* no evidence.

How far did I shoot? I heard it, so it can't have been far. I push myself back up and raise my torch high, scanning the roots where memory swears the telltale *splat* had come from. No trace of white. Not so much as a shine of moisture. Nothing but roots, sunk into loam.

Where did it go?

The uncanny sense that I am being watched pulls me away. As a lone bright thing in the dark, I'm vulnerable. I switch off my torch… go quiet. The air isn't suffocatingly warm anymore, but it tastes acrid. Almost smoky. Like kissing someone after they've had a cigarette.

It's late. I'm exhausted in every way a man can be. No wonder I'm thinking ridiculous things, feeling wholly irrational, unfounded fears. Like the fear that I am not alone.

That here, *I* am not the apex predator.

I'm not stupid, and I'm no gambler. Fears don't need to be rational for me to heed them when there's no reason *not* to. Memory guides me back toward camp. I trust it to put me in the right direction, but not to protect me from this labyrinth of rising and falling roots. I tread carefully, never trusting the foot moving forward enough to keep the other anything but firm on the ground. I still trip, losing the torch. I catch myself with both hands: one on the ground, the other on a tangled mass of roots as thick as my arm.

Something is warm beneath my palm. The roots shift and undulate at my touch. My heart rate shoots right back to where the memory of Shiloh had coaxed it minutes ago. The scientist in me reaches toward the thing while instinct warns me to flee. *Still warm.* The ripple against my hand is subtle and doesn't last long—but it is there, all right. Movement. Like something breathing? No.

Like the stiff throat of something *swallowing*.

Getting to camp is taking longer than it should. The air still has a taste. With that taste comes a strange, uncanny sense for the shape of things... the curvature of the earth beneath my feet. I find myself taking strange paths laid out by this omnipresent sprawl of massive roots. It's like navigating sidewalks that modernization had forcibly grafted onto an ancient, European city. I'm squeezed between a pair of closely huddled trees when there is plenty of space to either side, guided to move through rather than around deep puddles. Like I'm being funneled someplace. Led.

I lick my lips and taste a sugary sharpness. Only then does it occur to me to wonder if I'm even walking back toward camp at all. I pause to take stock of my surroundings, systematically charting my perimeter with torchlight. That light sputters out. Everything closes in on me at once.

"Shit." I give the thing a sharp jab with the heel of my hand. Two more jabs and it stutters back to life, illuminating a disruption in the root-tangled loam. A stretch of smooth, waxen beige in the green. Then, it's gone.

My own mind has been buzzing to fill the silence. Something else rises to join it. Distant thunder? No. Humming. The probably futile task of convincing my torch to cooperate continues, and so must I. I make it only a few steps before stumbling over something. My torch finally cooperates to reveal a boot: Val's.

I stay still and chart my way forward with torchlight before letting myself be led off again. Another boot plots the course to her jacket. Her trousers. Twin scraps of red that had once been her shirt. The humming is clearer now. Something like a melody peeks through in fits and starts, distorted by long stretches of strained, wheezing breath and silence... mutters... clacking teeth.

I don't know what state Val's in. I just know she's decided to make her way out here, possibly sleep-walking. Singing.

Singing *to* someone.

I've been holding my torch lightly like a pen. Now, I hold it with far more readiness. Like a weapon. I don't call out to her. I want to find her before she finds me. One of us is in our right mind, and it is clearly not Dr. Val Rowan. Bouncing LED light is a dead giveaway, unfortunately. I imprint my trajectory as best I can and switch it off. Hopefully, it will turn on when I need it to. Hope is hard to locate just now, though—not unlike my erstwhile and possibly demented colleague.

More humming. Chattering teeth. An empty, wet mouthing sound like someone pantomiming sucking a lozenge with nothing in their mouth but tongue. Or empty kissing. Between it all, more muttering. "I know that, sweetheart. Mommy knows." A shuddering wheeze. "Mommy knows it hurts. We know it hurts."

My muscles tense. Her murmured nonsense gets louder. Only once I've aimed the torch at the ground several meters away from me do I switch it on.

Val is there, standing before a large, vine-armored tree. Her face is turned from me, luckily enough. She's stripped down to her underwear to reveal her sagging places: stomach, cellulite-puckered inner thighs, stretch-mark laced breasts. An ugly, raised scar creeps across her lower abdomen. C-section, most likely. Unplanned. The unfired-terra-cotta shine of it catches my torchlight better than her eyes do. Her small hands cling lightly to the papery vines braided along the tree in front of her, like she's been dancing with it. Intimately.

The humming returns. No tune I recognize. No tune at all. Just musical babbling nonsense. When Val presses her mouth to the tree, the sound fades out once more. Even as my teeth press against my bottom lip to form Val's name, I say nothing. The same instinct that kept me from getting my arse kicked during research stints in less enlightened portions of the world keeps me silent now.

Val's words are deadened by the bark digging into her lips. "You're so good, sweetie," she whispers again and again, pressing her nose and forehead deeper into hard ridges, like an overly affectionate cat. "You're such a good boy. You're so good, sweetie. So good, so good. You're such a good boy. Mommy loves you so much… so much. So good… so good."

My instincts are sharp, but they have nothing on my curiosity. I walk closer and shine my torch directly on the base of the tree, slowly pushing it higher and higher. Light moves over Val's dirt-caked feet and shins… up her bare thighs… her dirt-streaked pants… along her brown arms, stopping at clawed hands, and the pale patch of bare wood beneath.

"Good lord." Her short nails are torn to shreds. Bits of her are doubtlessly embedded in the wood. Grooves like those a worm might have left once chart the looping circuit of her bloody grasping.

"Such a good boy," she whispers. Only then do I realize she's turned to me now, staring at me—pupils blown wide. No wonder I'd barely been able to make her eyes out in the darkness. They've gone practically black.

I draw up the stern voice of a professor quickly losing his patience. "*Val! Dr. Rowan!*" No reaction. She's still looking at me, but not really *seeing* me. Again, she nuzzles her cheek against the bark, lips loose like a half-asleep lover hoping for an accidental kiss in the night. I don't hear her well, but I just catch the tongued Ds in her words, see her ragged, swollen lips mouth, "So good... so good—"

Crack.

Val *slams* her face against the tree. I'm too shocked to move—powerless to do anything but watch her beatific, bleeding face crane back for round two.

The *snap* of a branch in the distance snaps me out of it. "For fuck's sake." I stride forward, grab her by the shoulders, spin her away from the tree she's determined to drill her way into, and give her a firm *slap* across the face.

Black eyes stare off in the direction my hand forced her gaze, mouth hanging open. Spit drips from her chin, thick and wet like a dog's. I pull my hand back again, ready.

Val croaks, "Where am I?"

"Roughly twenty meters from camp," I tell her, though I'm guessing. It's not that I hope we really are that close. It's my instinct that proximity to manmade things grants me some sort of advantage.

"Where?" she asks. "*Where*?"

"The Western Expanse." Her drooling hasn't stopped. Firmly, I demand, "Tell me your name."

Bark-torn lips tremble, then press together and open in slow pulsing motions, like a butterfly pumping its wings. She's about to cry. I didn't think Val knew how to cry. But no, she doesn't cry. She's just forming her answer.

And the answer she gives me is: "*Mommy*."

You don't spend hundreds of nights sleeping in the woods, desert, and swamps of the continent without learning the value of 1. a decent sedative, and 2. the friendship of a doctor willing to prescribe one, no questions asked. It takes enough drugs to knock out a mid-sized cow before Val stops trying to claw her way out of her tent and silence her damned wailing for her dead son or some such nonsense. From outside, I watch her silhouette for a long time, monitoring for signs of waking. Her pulse was fine last I checked. Breathing slow but steady enough.

Something's happening here. That much is certain. Was there some ulterior motive underlying a presumedly generous research opportunity from DTU? Could we have been drugged? When? We haven't even tapped into the Waypoint's cache of rations (seemed doubtful we'd be provided with vegan options). We even packed our own water filtration devices. Environmental causes, then? Most likely. Whatever the cause, it's possibly affected me too—but far less intrusively, less *violently* than it's affected her. Could a discrepancy in our body mass account for that? A hormonal difference perhaps?

Have we stumbled into the *true* reason the Western Expanse has been so stringently cordoned off with everything from barbed wire to assault towers? *Fucking hell.* We've been denied crucial information. All the samples we've collected to this point could well be compromised. This may have all been for naught. An entire gruelling month with *fuck-all* to show for it.

Heads will roll later. Now, I need to rest, recuperate, and be ready to get back to the security checkpoint ASAP. I can't carry Val. I don't know that getting her away from *whatever* is impacting her would bring her back to herself, whole and functioning. Leaving her behind may be the best course of action. I can go then come back with help far more quickly than I can shepherd a crazy woman through the Florida wilderness solo.

Nothing prowls these woods but us. She'll be fine on her own. I can pool our rations and leave her with a full two-weeks' worth. She'll hardly have to leave her tent if—

I freeze. Listening. The flap of Val's tent door flits in the wind, subtle as an owl's wings.

Her tent is empty.

"Fucking, fuck, fuck, *fuck.*"

Every fifth stride has me stumbling over these—*why are these fucking roots fucking everywhere?* With each misstep, my ungainly pack shifts and upsets my balance further but I do not care. I don't even bother with the stabilizing straps in case I need to break away in a hurry. I keep my pace up. There's no trail of discarded clothes to guide me this time, but I can only assume Dr. Batty has returned to the beloved tree where I found her. This time—probably because I'm not wrangling an insane woman—I notice something rather obvious on the ground.

A blinking red light.

Is that a bit of bone? Or maybe shell embedded in the dirt? I bend down to brush some soil aside, revealing silicone. It's an old-fashioned recording earpiece. I pry it up with a stick. The white silicone is as weathered and yellowed as a smoker's teeth. Voxnodes aren't a technology that's been in wide use for well over a decade, but this battery is still running strong. It only takes a bit of fiddling to get the thing to play back. Static distorts the first saved file. I skip forward until something other than hissing white noise comes through:

"Dictation," a woman says, her voice dim. "Doctor Ismene Nakamura, Professor of Natural Philosophy and Robert F. Kennedy Chair of Wildlife, DTU. April 1st, 2055, 16:30." A long pause. She continues, "Correction: Precise time unknown—" Another pause. Then, a muffled, percussive sound. Two taps. "I've located what appears to be—" Another two taps. Nakamura's frustration is unmistakable now. "A specimen—*no!*"

A startled gasp crackles in my palm. Brushing, feather-edged sounds. Her breath is audible now.

Nothing.

I'm about to skip ahead when she whispers, "What in the—"

Rustling. Motion.

"I didn't know what they would do. I didn't *know*."

Strained breathing. A faint, plaintive noise. "I made a mistake. I was *scared* and I made a mistake, I'm *sorry*. I am. But I have a family, Cherisé—" A rasp edges her breathing as it speeds up. "Oh, God, I am so sorry, I meant—I meant *Charlie*, I swear, you know I've never done that before, you know I haven't, you know that's not who I am"—her words take on a manic tone: so fast, they're difficult to parse out—"I would never. I would *never*, I—" A long, wheezing, choked-off inhale.

A wheezing breath out, a shallow breath in.

In, out... in, out... in, out... then, silence.

I wait. Faint hums emerge. Muffled groans. The sounds get louder, more distressed. Like she's covered her mouth with her hand to silence her sobs—her fear. Those sounds become rhythmic. Intentional.

Whatever follows isn't human. It's far too mechanical. Precise. Back and forth, back and forth—like someone sawing through wood.

Finally, what I can only assume to be Nakamura returns with a wet, gurgling groan of sheer *relief*. A heavy thud.

There is nothing else.

Silence returns.

I stand there a long time, staring at the device in my palm. I scoff at myself. What was I expecting? Instruction? Advice? I hardly needed to be told that something deeply *fucked up* is happening here. All I have is more questions and fewer answers. I need to get out of here. I can't be any help to Rowan if I wind up in a similar state. The logical thing to do is *leave*.

At this point I'm not even looking for Rowan, but I keep my ears piqued for insane woman sounds. With every minute's hurried walk toward the border, the air feels less oppressive. Welcoming, even. I can't smell my own panicked stink anymore, just a light, floral, earthy sort of smell. A crisp, pleasant night. Maybe the relief of a decision, of a p*lan forward*, has finally let my brain notice how pleasant this place can be at night. Even the breeze is at my back, helping me onward. It reaches the sweat on my neck and arms and washes over me with pleasant tingles. I lick my lips to feel it there too.

I do. I do feel it. Taste it, too. That sharp sweetness is back.

I lick my lips again. I need that breeze more than ever. It's warm. Hot. Christ, I'm already starting to sweat again. I shimmy out of my pack to peel off my outer layers. The humming is back, but it isn't Val's. Something properly musical. Quiet but steady. As I tune in, the melody collects into a word.

"Professor?"

Only when something trips me do I realize I've stepped toward the sound. I'd tripped on a shirt—mine? I touch the sweat-damp hair below my navel to confirm it. When did I take it off? My hand falls lazily, listlessly to my waistband to toy with the elastic there.

Less confirming so much as willing him into existence, I say, "Shiloh?"

Whatever else may be true of my mind, the flesh is still weak.

I'm dreaming. Must be. That is far more plausible than Rowan managing to run off so heavily drugged. I'm no stranger to lucid dreaming: controlling my nocturnal world. This all feels too strange, too distant to be real—like a miniature ocean world contained behind aquarium glass. The forest *looks* like a dream, but it *feels* like reality. I can taste the heavy wetness of the air. Feel the subtle crackle of hairs rising on my neck, the rise of blood to my throat and face. I smell the deep, acrid bite of soil and something almost like gasoline. Or coal. Something that shouldn't be there. Wild onions? No. Wild onions are another flowering species lost in the SMEE.

But then, why not? What meaning has death in a dream?

The brush of hot air on my inner wrist is as there, as visceral as any waking touch. Again, I incant the name, "Shiloh."

And there he is. Waiting for me. How he was always waiting for me. Leaning against that huge, vine-tangled tree, smooth pale legs folded beneath him, arms crossed just so to hide the scars on his chest. As if I won't pry those arms apart and expose them myself once I get there. Dark blonde hair falls into his eyes and over his ears, blending into pitiful, boyish peach fuzz.

Round brown eyes look anywhere but at my own while I unbuckle my belt. He looks as if he's about to take a punishment. I suppose I must look like I'm about to give him one. I don't bother pushing my trousers any further than it takes to draw out my cock before giving it an easy stroke. There's no need; it's already hot and heavy in my hand.

Shiloh's eyes drop to my feet, and I kick my trousers off entirely. He doesn't make a sound when I push his knees apart to kneel between them, but he does let me. His eyes move up, lingering on my cock with something almost like surprise. Wonderment.

Adorable.

I can smell how wet he is—can already taste the sharp saltiness of him. It's so precious the way he always insists he doesn't want it in his pussy. They almost always do.

They almost always give in, too.

Shiloh doesn't resist my weight, doesn't make a sound. Not until I slide inside. He whimpers then. I pin him to the dirt like a butterfly, and when it beats its wings I only go deeper. He makes for such a decadent display. A painting. A sculpture. A warm, beating ode to man's mastery over nature.

"Such a good boy," I growl in his ear, fucking him harder—deep enough that every rough punch against his cervix makes his body convulse in a prelude to doubling over, like he's just taken a punch to the gut. His belly-deep groans sound like it, too.

I lick him from scarred chest to ear while I rock against him, relishing the smoothness of him. He tastes sweet, how I've always imagined real, earth-grown peaches might taste. Far sweeter, riper than they had any need to be. Wanton. I bite into his flesh to carve myself into his neck. His thighs twitch against my ribs while he rasps out his pleas for something I can't hear over the roar of blood in my ears. Doesn't matter. I'm nearly finished.

I need to see him. I need to see his face the moment he understands he's full of me now. That I've claimed the deepest, most shameful parts of him. Remind him just how quickly he gave in to this, how badly he really, truly wanted it. For Darwin, reproduction is the highest good. Shiloh could cry all he wanted about it, make histrionics about his life being ruined, but deep down we both knew the truth: he wanted it.

He needed to be that highest good for me.

I need to see how beautifully he breaks.

Shiloh's eyes are clenched shut like a child waiting to be woken from a nightmare. I grip his hips tighter and tell him, "Open your eyes." Of course he does. Shiloh's freckles shift color in the light, giving him the appearance of something I've dragged out from the sea. An erstwhile creature of myth caught in my net—helpless to do anything but please me.

My saliva drips like syrup at the sight of it, pooling in that delicate clavicle. The place I'd bitten glows deep and red, fresh as a wound. Tender. Raw. I lick it and taste heat and its sweetness just makes my mouth water even more. My own moans surprise me, but I don't stop. Each sucking, biting kiss at Shiloh's neck draws fresh whimpers. Petal-soft heels dig into my ass, pulling me deeper. He actually feels warmer, *tighter* now.

The hot pull of his insides tugs at me from the inside out. My mouth hangs open, panting against his neck as I'm helpless to do anything but thrust my way deeper, chasing that exquisite tension on the edge of pain. "*Fuck.*" I've got just enough control to lean back and watch his baby face break. Brown eyes stay open, as ordered. Mouth, soft and pink as a long-extinct flower stays open too. His breath smells fragrant and sweet. Like tea. Like honey. Like a world more beautiful and caring than this one, where birds and bees and bugs and bats can guard against the silence.

Short fingernails dig into my back, urging me to stay inside him even as his eyes water with the silent effort of begging me to do anything else. I tell him I'm close just to hear him whimper—hear that feigned chastity these boys are always so, so good at. I grab his arms and pin both wrists above his head with one hand, bracing myself on his hip with the other. Each of my staccato thrusts gets nothing more than a hollow sound—not a vocalization of the mouth. A sound forced out from his gut.

Between pants, I grunt out, "Such a good boy—" and tense my glutes, ready to fuck every drop of my cum into that perfect pussy, deep as it'll go. But before I can chase my climax, something slows me down. I go still. A hot breeze ghosts over my back, tingling the sweat that's pooled above my ass. My left hand's still pinning Shiloh's hands down. I give his fingers a squeeze, expecting a soft squeeze back. Instead, I find something rough and brittle with the wrong sort of give. Not the give of supple flesh. The give of something hollow. His hand crumples at my touch like an origami bird.

Shiloh whimpers again, but now it echoes in his narrow ribcage—or from the ground beneath it—alternating between human sounds and something split into an octave. First two, then three rasping notes.

"Shiloh?" I whisper urgently. His mouth is bigger. A once plaintive pout has stretched wide, falling downward into a frown every bit as dramatic, inhuman as a tragic mask. *I can't make out any teeth.* Then, where wrinkles would have formed if Shiloh'd lived past twenty-three, four seams appear in an X across his face, deep and red like freshly knit cuts.

I make to touch one. Something stops me. A sharp sensation straddling a knife's edge between pleasure and pain. Only moments ago, Shiloh's tight heat had been coaxing my release from me—tugging at my balls, readying me to fill him. Now, that same tug isn't being pulled out.

It's being pushed back *in*.

I know then. I *know* I am not dreaming.

"*Fuck!*" Something's poking its way into my urethra. "Shiloh," I whisper hurriedly, "There's—" I stop short. The two lines of Shiloh's clenched-shut eyes have broken apart and spread to twist themselves into a dozen new openings. A honeycomb of stomata stare back at me. Dozens of misshapen black holes have replaced his eyes: infinitely deep, infinitely empty. Then, Shiloh's face *splits* along the seams. Corners unfurl and peel back to reveal muscle, raw and red—but it's wrong. All wrong. The fibers are running in the wrong direction, not following the contours of the face. Each one springs outward from the black hole of his toothless, contorted mouth. That mouth expands, widening.

Deepening.

Something's pushing its way inside my dick while Shiloh blooms open beneath me. His entire body groans like wood freezing and expanding in winter. It sounds inhuman but not artificial. Organic. Utterly unbothered by me furiously trying to tug my root-bound hand away. My left hand is bound now, lashed to the ground by the gray-sheathed burgundy roots of something warm and pulsing and alive.

Shiloh's arms and legs have flushed a deep,

purple-red; they're freckled in black. Under my horrified gaze, the freckles drill their way down, perforating him with hundreds of deep holes. Dark veins, thick and labyrinthine, follow the contours of his limbs. All lead to the still-expanding maw that's swallowed the heart of him. Glassy drops of deep, dark red bleed out from those stomata dotting his flesh. No, not flesh. The thing's fully unfurled now. What I'm looking at—what I'm *tethered* to—is a massive plant. An epiphyte. The monstrous *orchid* that's been parasitizing this tree and now has transferred its death-grip to *me*. I stare down into the whorl of darkness where Shiloh's face—what I'd *mistaken* for Shiloh's face—had been.

My scientific curiosity is short-lived. Any questions other than *How do I break away without destroying myself? How do I make it stop? Am I going to die here?* disappeared the moment something started snaking its way inside me. I manage to wrench my hand from the roots above and lean back. The moment I get to my knees, I feel like I'm pissing something hot and thick—far thicker than my body was made to accommodate. Pain clenches my thighs, and I go desperately still, terrified to move anything but my eyes.

God help me, but I am more terrified to move my eyes than anything. I still look down.

My "*Oh god*" breaks into a choked sob.

One fleshy pink root as thick as a pen has wormed its way inside my dick. Fine, dark red hairs glint with each subtle ripple of motion along the length of it. The same glossy red liquid I'd sucked at so greedily before lubricates the way inside me. I swallow down my panic, forcing my breathing to slow. I need to keep my head. Stay in your mind, I repeat to myself again and again as I study the rest of the root with my eyes. It just gets thicker, and thicker, and thicker. After only twelve inches, the thing's already as thick as my own turgid penis.

And it's inching deeper. Stretching me wider. Fucking me from the inside out.

I claw at my crotch and force myself not to thrash away, terrified of ripping something inside me. My hand presses harder, trying to stall the root from creeping in any farther. It's squirming within me, undaunted by my grip, pulsing against my palm—unless that's my own dick. It's still swollen, still filled, still red and filled to bursting and just getting redder, hotter to the touch.

A musky smell swells up—so thick I can taste it, and it tastes *warm*. I can't help myself. My hips start to rock, matching the root motion for motion, fucking myself onto it. Some deep recess of me recognizes my actions are being manipulated, but that knowledge can't touch the urge to fuck myself deeper.

The flesh is so, so fucking weak.

One red petal-like arm (or arm-like petal?) coils around my wrist and yanks it down, forcing me to the side and pinning me there. The vine moves inside me while I can only watch it shift and ripple, subtle like muscle beneath flesh. Penetrating me. It's past the base of my dick now. I can feel it following the curved paths of me, searching something out. A stab into my prostate has me twitching against my restraints, spasming with every sharp touch. Then that vine splits in two and my world splits open— paroxysms of pain and pleasure tear each other apart, feeding on each other.

My orgasm is ripped from me like raw meat off a bone.

The vine outside me bulges and quakes, sucking me down. Messily. Something oozes out of me: first pink, then red-streaked white. Now only red. The vine settles. Thousands of fine hairs shimmer and rustle, like hair gently stroked along the grain... and then against it. Bristling. I can smell the change. It's as sudden and palpable as the drop in air pressure heralding a massive storm. The air's turned hazy, the colors distorted. It has a taste. Sulfurous.

The nectar that had been oozing, slick and generous from the petals has coagulated to muddy blobs. Smaller drops crack under my gaze. They crumble when the petals shift, leaving behind dusty streaks of pink. Something's sliding up my sweaty back, charting a back-and-forth path like a snake. Another root. It lashes around my neck and forces my head back. My spine cracks at the sudden shift in angle when it tugs me down to the ground, pressing me against its central cluster where the roots are thickest.

Footsteps behind me. I try to crane my head,

but I can't move. It's only once the source steps into my field of vision that I see Val Rowan.

She's still naked, nose bruised and broken. Dried blood cakes her mouth. I might even think she'd been gorging on cherries if I hadn't watched her tear up her lips myself.

I frown at her pink-stained teeth. She's smiling.

"Val?"

She smiles wider. Far more sweetly than I've ever heard her say anything, she whispers, "*Such* a good boy."

The last thing I see is the golden glint of my own fountain pen.

The last thing I hear is just how weak my flesh really is.

"That Flowers Would Bloom": Plant Creativity and the Agential Limitations of Intelligence

by Orion Rael Armijo, in partial fulfillment for the Ph.D. in Ecology (Botany)

CALIFORNIA NATIONAL UNIVERSITY

Advisor: Joy Soto, Ph.D.

Like its author, this dissertation does not exist separately from the ecosystem from which it springs. I am imbricated with and indebted to far too many people to list here, but that's no reason not to try.

Firstly, I'd like to thank Dr. Joy Soto for agreeing to step up as my advisor for the final stretch when circumstances necessitated it. Her involvement was brief but impactful. My correspondence with Dr. Sophie del Toro was indispensable. I am indebted to her not only for her veritable library of bibliographic suggestions, but also her kind encouragement. I met Hannah Plumwood at my first Sierra Club event a decade ago, but she's never once wavered in her generosity, patience, and humor. I couldn't ask for a better reader than her.

Naturally, this work has been heavily shaped and influenced by my original advisor, Dr. Leon Angelo, without whom this dissertation would not be possible. His decades of work were foundational to this project. I am indebted to him for his tutelage during my tenure at California National University.

The Unblooming but not Forgotten Foundation funded six months of research in both the Pecos Wilderness and Adirondack Forest Preserve which served as the basis for chapters 3 and 4, and the Graduate Division generously provided me with a fellowship without which this dissertation would not have been possible.

~~Last and most, this monstrosity survives at the mercy of my best friend, Zoë. Your dad jokes and floral puns got me through the process of formatting my bibliography. Your insights made this work stronger, but your oatmeal cookies and chili-mac made life worth surviving.~~

Part III: *Synomone*

Human necks did not evolve to do this.

Wincing, I peel my cheek off a sweat-damp forearm. The other man in bed with me—his bed, not mine—is also naked, splayed out on his back. Narrow hips do their best to roll away from me. The moment it's free, the tanned and toned left arm that had been "supporting" me relocates to a shaved ball sack. I was less something to be held onto so much as something in the way of him scratching himself. Shocker.

Projected green numbers on the ceiling tell me it's almost eight. Class starts at nine. *Goddamnit.* I crack my fingers and stretch my arms in front of me with a groan. The tattooed words spanning my knuckles are as much a question as an accusation at times like these: on the left, NATURE, on the right, NURTURE. I let my hands fall to the stretch of olive-brown skin beneath my own navel, fingers ghosting over the fine black hair there. It feels cool to the touch. Some inches below, though, feels hot. Not like pleasure. How a fresh slap feels hot. An insult that cut just a little too close to the truth.

Something alien is churning in there—a sack of hot liquid worms, all squirming to tunnel deeper. I've left a wet, terra cotta patch on the middle of the mattress. It's not even red enough to look like blood. Not thick enough, alive enough, to retain its diluted brownish color all the way to the edges. Instead, the stain just spreads in a halo of colorless wet. I probably won't even get blamed for it. Nothing about that stain suggests *fresh*. Or even *alive*.

Something dead left that stain there. If it can even be considered a stain at all. Anything alive enough to leave a permanent mark was all *him*.

At least I had the sense to wind up on the side where I left the vodka. I never even bother jerking myself off after these guys fall asleep anymore. Not sure why I bother with anything at this point, but I'm not blowing this much of my pitiful adjunct salary on alcohol (et al) for the sake of introspection. I don't have to go looking for anything but my clothes, so I've got that going for me. Once upon a time, I might've brought along a prosthetic: a higher-end one. Far too expensive for either of us. I don't bother anymore. Even the guys the apps match me with because my profile said "top" and theirs said "vers bottom" act like it's *cute* when I suggest using it:

I just hate the feel of silicone, you know? That's okay, right? It's just easier if I fuck you, right? Wouldn't that be more convenient? I mean, your hole is made for it, right? I mean, risking pregnancy and the whole medical Rube Goldberg machine of trauma that would follow isn't more inconvenient than me having to douche, right? I hate the feel of latex and polyurethane even more than silicone, baby boy, but I swear on my mom's life I'll pull out!

Yeah, fucking fine. Sure. Whatever.

Every cis dude swears on his mother's life he'll pull out. They usually don't. Not for me, at least. That's not on them. That's on me. You can't change other people's actions, just your own. Yet here I am: the asshole hoping his way into insanity again and again and again. I really used to hate that quote people drop all the time—attributed to Einstein, usually—defining insanity as doing the same thing over and over and expecting a different result. Not just because it's trite. Because it's incorrect. There's some real unfortunate truth in there, but it leaves out a crucial step. It's not that doing the same thing over and expecting a different result is insane. It's doing the same thing over and over and *daring to hope* for a different result that's insane. But only because holding hope in times like these, in a world like that, in a body like *this* that makes hope absolutely fucking insane.

Sure that's bleak. But I'm not the one who made it that way.

I swing my legs over the edge of the bed and take a swig of vodka so I don't have to think too hard about how parts I wish I didn't even *have* are full of entitled-asshole cum. Naturally, it's not me pulling away from his half-assed embrace, or my hunched shoulders and blank face that gets this guy's attention. It's the dribbling sound of liquor sloshing onto his stupid fucking Keith Haring carpet. Not like the vodka's got any more power to stain that white poly blend than I've got to stain Asher or Ethan or Ashen over here. Just one more evolutionary advantage he's got over me, I guess.

"What the fuck are you doing?" he demands.

I don't stop, don't look at him. I just keep staring at the twisting glass stream and answer in the Texan drawl I'm too tired to mask anymore. "Pouring one out for all the dead mothers."

"Just how old do you fuckers think I am, exactly?"

"I don't know, like, forty?"

To be fair, that's only seven years off. Maybe six. Eight? Who the fuck can keep track after thirty? I'm way too hung over for this. And I'm pretty sure Mason or Axel or Maxim or whoever the fuck gave me an STI. My pelvis pangs like somebody in cowboy boots just kicked me in my psychic balls. I should've just stayed a lesbian. The father of botany was a Lesbian man—why not me?

From the back of the classroom, another student chimes in with "It was before our time!" like it helps.

I all-but-shriek, "So was *Charles Darwin!* You've heard of *him*, right?" Blank looks. "If nobody says, 'Yes' in the next seven seconds, you *all* fai—"

"Yes," comes the flat chorus.

"Look," I say, pointing a stern finger at the tech-board. "Put your Gen-Gamma snark away and pay attention, this is import—"

Twig, a junior in the front row asks, "Will it be on the final, Professor Armijo?" before rapidly correcting, "Sorry, I mean Professor *Or*—I mean *'just Orion?'*"

"Yeah! It's gonna be on the fucking final, Twig!" Twig (infuriatingly enough) is trying very hard not to laugh. The thought of being a role model nauseates me, but trans elders aren't exactly easy to come by, and I'm the only one I know of in these parts.

"What, really? The exam's next week!"

"Really! I cannot in good conscience let any of you graduate with a degree from this esteemed-adjacent institution of so-called learning before you understand this." I clear my throat. "Right. Back to the 1998 masterpiece *Godzilla*. Matthew Broderick of *Ferris Bueller's Day Off* fame—"

"What's Ferris—"

"F's. All of you. F's." Now that my tirade's been punctuated with the standard threat, I feel like a tourist in duck floaties who puts his glasses back on only to realize he's drifted way farther out to sea than he'd intended. "Where was I?"

Ferdinand obliges. "Plant judgment."

"Yes! Plants. Judgment. Do they have it? That is, when presented with options for action and reaction, do plants choose the most sensible course?"

A few noses wrinkle at different points: Valeria at "action," Hugh and Noelani at "choose." Xorie's nose wrinkles at "reaction," but that may just be a sneeze coming on. 2061 and still the world is not replete of skeptics.

"Okay," I say slowly, "I lost you on the whole 'plant agency' thing. But what if…" I trail off, searching. There's a can of electronic cleaning spray under the podium; I grab it. Then, a pen and lint-removal roller from Noelani's bag. I ignore her halfhearted "*Hey?*" before continuing, "Say"—I dump the items onto Jenn's desk—"Jenn, here, is being attacked by ladybugs. They're eating her right up. So, Jenn, what do you do?"

"Nothing," Jenn says, figurative pearls a-clutch at the very notion. "If there are any ladybugs around then they are incredibly endangered!"

I stare at her. "I like where your head's at, Jenn, but you can't damage the ecosystem by curb-stomping hypothetical bugs." To the class at large, I continue, "Jenn, handily enough, has evolved certain tools. She's got… this, um, sticky thing? This noxious spray stuff"—at the push of a button, an acrid-smelling puff of air hisses out—"and that-there sharp pokey thing. Congrats, Jenn. Good job evolving."

Jenn beams. "Thanks!"

Xorie sneezes, and Jenn says, "Blessed be," while I pretend to teach some more: "Pre-SMEE, plants could communicate with their environments through—what?"

Four hands shoot up; I call on Roz. "Semiochemicals." At my look, she elaborates. "Plants can, um… not '*channel*—'"

Noelani suggests, "Synthesize?"

"Right, thanks! Plants can *synthesize* chemical compounds that communicate, like, messages and stuff?" Roz stops. My brows go up, expectant. She tiptoes on. "To… other plants around them?" My brows go up higher, more expectant. Dawning realization lights up her face. "But not just other *plants*. Animals, too."

"Excellent! What does that have to do with Jenn and her special botanical toolkit? Assume *this* stuff"—I hold up the can—"contains *semiochemicals*. Any guesses on what kind?" *Nada.* "Welp, if *y'all* were being eaten to death by *Coccinellidae*, what would you *want* your semiochemicals to do?"

"Um…" Siobhan's voice is barely audible in the back row. Her hand is only raised high enough that she can't pretend like she'd just meant to brush her hair behind her ear at the last second. "I'd want the spray to tell the ants to stop?"

"Smart! Manipulating the behavior of other individuals makes *this humble can* a specific type of semiochemical called a"—I put it up on the techboard—"*allomone*. What else? Any other allomone strategies?" Brains are working, but nothing's manifesting but barely masked frustration and preemptive disappointment. "Ladybugs are eating you," I prompt. "Are ladybugs the apex predator in these parts?"

Noelani's hand shoots up. "Ooh! The semiochemicals could say, like, 'Hey, anybody who thinks ants are tasty, come over here!'"

"Yes!"

Gretchen shakes her head with what might be abject confusion or wonder. "No way. No way plants can do that, that's *insane*."

"Insane *and* true. How fucking rad is that?" The fact that most students seem to concede that this is indeed *fucking rad* restores my faith in humanity by roughly 4%. "You already know that scientists started picking up on just how complex plants were pre-SMEE. Whispers of 'plant intelligence' were popping up in the twentieth century, even. It wasn't until after pollution levels and climate change got so bad that plants went effectively mute, that we really started to appreciate just how deeply embedded they were in their environments, their communities, and *how* they were embedded in those communities: through a kind of language. Semiotics. But instead of *words*, they used *chemicals*."

Twig sinks in his seat. "Oh! *Semiochemicals*."

Siobhan's face, meanwhile, is a dramatic mask of confusion. "But plants can't *do stuff*. They're *plants*."

"No?" I counter, tossing the spray can in my hand. "There was a whole class of plants called myrmecophytes—write that down—also known as ant-loving plants that formed…." Bruce is resplendent with *are-you-fucking-kidding-me?* energy. "Fair enough. M.Y.R.M.E.C.O.P.H.Y.T.E.S. Myrmecophytes formed symbiotic relationships with a *particular* colony of ant, exuding nectar just for them. Like domestication. So, if *another* bug starts nibbling on their leaves, they—" I give the can a quick spray—"like Noelani suggested, call in their buds, and they come charging in because they're not about to lose their favorite all-you-can-eat nectar buffet. Clever, right?" I place the can back on my desk with a *thunk.* "Conversations don't move in just one direction though, do they? You can't have just one speaker. Those bugs eating the plant? The plant is *listening* to them—figuratively speaking. By interpreting saliva, it knows exactly what is attacking it."

Several students chorus, "What?"

"Yeah," I confirm. "These plants figure out who is eating their leaves, then—one could argue— *make a judgment* of what to do next. A particular, rational course of action followed, at any rate. Basically, they read 'caterpillar' while they were being actively eaten, and *because* of that, they would deploy semiochemicals to summon the wasps that attack *those precise caterpillars.*"

Siobhan has stopped taking notes altogether. She's just staring at me like I just told her microwaving vodka removes half the calories.

"Other plants," I go on, "could change their

own chemical makeup in ways we *still* can't understand, let alone *synthesize*—and they'd do this on the *fly*. That same nectar that was oh-so tasty a second ago? Well, now it glues that hungry hungry caterpillar's mouth shut so it *can't* chew on that plant anymore." After a beat, I add, "Or... on anything else ever again." A few students stare back at me, horrified. One looks attentive but somewhat lost, so I add, "The caterpillars starve to death, Orlando." This doesn't help. "What is it, buddy?"

Orlando asks, "What did this have to do with Godzilla?"

Uncharacteristically insightful question. What *does* this have to do with Godzilla? Not that one *needs* a reason to bring up Godzilla, but—

"Um, Orion?" Jenn offers a timid smile and an assist. "You were talking about Darwin? And the Star Orchid? And how Mothra—"

"Right! *Thank you.* So, based on this orchid's unusually long nectary tube—where an insect's proboscis accesses nectar—Darwin hypothesized that there must exist a moth with a foot-long proboscis, far bigger than anything they'd ever encountered. So, what did this have to do with Mothra?" *Hungover teacher tip #41: reformulate lessons as questions so they teach themselves.*

Twig has already run through this calculus—probably had ages ago. "If a giant moth like Mothra exists, then we can hypothesize a flower with a nectary tube big enough to accommodate it?"

"Bingo. And before you ask, yes: Mothra

pollination is absolutely going to be on the final."

The deceptively innocuous *bing* of my tablet pierces the grumbling chorus. It's a message from my department chair: *SEE ME ASAP*. A stampede is on the move in the plaza outside. Class was meant to be over six minutes ago. "The fuck, Sophie? You had *one job*."

A sophomore in the second row gives me a sheepish smile. "Sorry. I was trying to pay attention 'cause you said it'd be on the final? So I could, you know, learn and stuff?"

"Okay, two jobs." I rub one hand over my eyes and wave the other at the door. "See you at the exam."

Infuriatingly enough, I catch several smiles—maybe even genuine ones—among the departing students. I'd expect freshman to find me entertaining. When you're fresh out of secondary, the collegiate discovery that *teachers can swear* (and be supremely hungover) is just one short step below the profundity of the realization that if what you *want* to eat for breakfast every day for the next four years is Oreos and methamphetamine, nobody can really stop you.

God can and probably will. But your R.A.'s really couldn't give fewer shits.

This meeting doesn't seem to be the coal-dragging I'd been anticipating. And, for some unholy reason, an official, CNU-library bound copy of my never-defended dissertation is laid out on Juniper's desk. Foil letters down the spine read:

"That Flowers Would Bloom": Plant Creativity and the Agential Limitations of Intelligence
    by Orion Rael Armijo, in partial fulfillment for the Ph.D. in Ecology (Botany)
    CALIFORNIA NATIONAL UNIVERSITY
    Advisor: Leon Angelo, Ph.D.

I never ordered a copy for myself. Didn't want to look at it—or, the one name Grad Division refused to amend. I still don't, actually, so I stop looking at it and take in the world-weary look on the department chair's face instead. Juniper Rubio is department chair only very, very reluctantly. I'm not old enough (or tenured enough) to have that problem. I *am* too old to be teaching a 6/6 course load, however, yet here we are: languishing in the worst possible timeline where climate change became irreversible and trans humanity remains a *matter of opinion* on much of the continent. Why can't we just have nice things? We should be taking teleportation machines to commute to Mars by now—for kicks. Robots should be doing all the adjuncting labor for us, freeing us up to paint landscapes and write poetry while riding the cough-syrup-and-antihistamine wave.

"—wife was very impressed."

Some point after bumping into a recycling

bin but right before knocking on Juniper's office door, I'd begun to worry that the antihistamine/cough syrup combo wasn't doing it for me. No need. That definitely sounded like the end of a paragraph, and I did not catch one starting. "What are you saying?"

"I'm saying," Juniper repeats(?) slowly, "that an FRF organization is offering funding and visa sponsorship for field research. The chair of the board—who is also the president's wife—is familiar with your work on plant creativity. She read your dissertation, and was very intrigued that you took the concept of plant intelligence and didn't just accept it as given, but took it that much further. Ascribed something like aesthetic sensibility."

Ignoring the question of how she even managed to get a copy, I say, "Yes, it made quite an impression at PBAC too."

"So did you."

If by 'impression,' Juniper means *double-fisted beers at the conference opening reception until I couldn't remember why the sight of my Ph.D. advisor made me want to punch the butterfly ice sculpture in the proboscis (or find my hotel room)*, she's right. I did very much do that. Her pinched expression tells me, yes: that is exactly what she'd meant by 'impression.' Regardless, the offer persists. "The purpose of the grant is to aid researchers in locating a particular orchid. It's rumored to be still blooming."

The notion of an orchid blooming—in

Florida—isn't even the most absurd part to my pickled brain. "I'm not a field researcher, I'm a historian," I remind her. "Hence the *mausoleum of books* I keep having to convince the custodial staff aren't a fire hazard every semester." They absolutely are, though. In fairness to books, some of the blame has to go to vodka. I realize that doesn't help my case, but I am a scientist by training, and that is salient information.

With a half-sad, half-affectionate smile, Juniper says, "That's how I know you were one of Leon's students. He was always so insistent on how crucial it is to fall in love with one's work. To hold it in your hands and feel the—"

"Yeah," I cut in. "Professor Angelo was real keen on holding scholastic hands."

Juniper was a student along with Angelo at Oxford. His equal. I was his T.A. and student. His subordinate. Our memories of the man are very, very different. *She* remembers the young man who shone as bright as a star and helped redefine a field in the midst of global existential turmoil. *I* remember the predator-in-sheep's-clothing with the weird Darwinian hangup, and FTM fetish with a penchant for less-than-consensual breeding—also, breath play.

It's way too fucking warm in here. My persisting consciousness is worrisome. The cough syrup/antihistamine combo is not performing so hot after all. Am I just developing tolerances far faster these days? Maybe my walking HR complaint of an advisor was right: Evolution really is speeding up.

Juniper says, "You assisted editing *Between the Shadow and the Soul*, correct?"

I bite back a grimace and nod, silent. I did far more than *assist in editing*, not that I got credit.

"I expect you've already heard, but there's already talk of making that work the topic of his memorial conference next—"

"Huh?" I cut in. "A who-what-now conference?"

"Memorial conference?" Juniper repeats, confusion plain. "For Leon?"

The news flushes the skin of my throat and shoulders in a way that hurts. A purely visceral sensation. Instinctive. Too immediate, too deep to identify an originating cause, and I've got no intention of chasing it down. Some roots are better left unexamined, some scabs best left undisturbed.

Juniper's face goes waxen. "You didn't know that Leon passed away. Technically, he's only presumed, but... you didn't know?"

"No. I did not."

"I am *so sorry!* I assumed you knew—that someone at CNU would have contacted you."

They might have done. Probably *did,* actually. But I've been working pretty hard at not having to remember how that man and that place exist since fleeing to the high desert, so I really couldn't say. I just can't.

I can't say anything at all.

My apartment is a place for me and my clothes to sleep, but also a halfway home for troubled plants and botanical rehabilitation center. I like to think of myself as a foster dad: one of the competent but cool ones they send the really traumatized plants to. This potted orchid I'm tending to now was left outside the Philosophy Department wing of all places. No wonder it's so miserable. Very rare to find this species outside the wild. Poor thing is a tangled mass of water-logged roots that make a pathetic *squish* in my hand. I wring it out like a sponge. Half these roots need to be cut away, if not more. "They'll grow back," I tell the plant as I start snipping. "I hope."

I could trick her into growing her roots faster or shift her resources to producing pseudobuds instead of foliage. All it takes is some environmental adjustment—a bit like tricking my body into producing more hair by injecting hormones. I won't though. She'll have to be quarantined. No telling what nasties might have carved a home for themselves there in that godforsaken hall of so-called *thinkers.* I take stock of the veritable greenhouse of an apartment around me, then stick her in a small patch of hallway that still gets some sunlight. There's not really anywhere to go but the wall, though. Oh well: What's one more hole? I shift books and folders to exhume a drill from roughly two-dozen layers of scholarly detritus. My security deposit is as good as gone, but that's a small price for orchid rights.

After an hour's less-than-graceful work, the epiphyte is mounted to the wall. I spray what remains of her roots; in moments, papery gray sheathes turn green. So does the wall, but that's a problem for my landlord. Wonder what that kid was hoping to get from this orchid? What the orchid failed to give them? Beauty, maybe? Orchids haven't claimed to give that for decades now. A sense of purpose? Charity? Something to care for? Or just something to break up the daily monotony?

I have a theory that every human being was traumatized in their youth by a story. For my brother, it was the 2041 live-action reboot (not to be confused with the 2029 and 2035 versions) of *Bambi.* Fairly standard. For me, it was a book— twentieth century. *The Giving Tree* by Shel 'Girl, you okay?' Silverstein. Story goes like this: Tree falls for a boy, gives him everything it has and gets nothing in return until it's just a stump for the boy's wrinkly ass to sit on. I couldn't get over that book for years, and I'm not the only one. Late nights in dive bars introduced me to three people with egos the size of sequoias and self-awareness the size of acorns who'd claimed kinship with the stump. One woman had a tattoo and everything.

I don't identify with the tree. I don't even understand it. I understand it less every time I look out my window at a bare horizon and see a forest of ghosts. Outside my ground-floor apartment is an endless monotony of pinkish beige ground and blue sky. Bushy bundles of chamisa are all that break up an otherwise flat stretch of rock and sand. Chamisa's always had the stubbornness of a weed. That's likely how it survived first, the severance in communication from its pollinators, and then the extinction of them—by reforming itself into flowerless stalks dependent entirely on the wind and luck to reproduce. Colorless. Unremarkable. Beholden to no one but air.

Flowers evolved to make themselves beautiful, desirable to pollinators. Now, those pollinators are gone. So is the beauty. Rye saw the opportunity in making itself appeal to humans and ultimately domesticated itself before it occurred to us to cultivate it. The question scientists still can't answer—the question that became my advisor-turned-lover's white whale—is: Why won't the flowers bloom for *us*?

I understand why. I do. I can't explain it in terms academics will accept, and I could never, *never* hope to explain it in terms that Leon could *hear*, let alone entertain. But I understand.

I understand why flowers stopped blooming for us.

There's this optical illusion I used to play around with. A drawing. Depending on how you look at it, it's either a duck or a rabbit. My mind could never commit to either. It still can't. Instead, I'm just sitting on my apartment floor in my boxers and an oversized hoodie, staring at my closed laptop, cognition rapidly vacillating between two images.

Duck. I should contact someone. Someone at CNU. Someone else affected, somebody else who'd gotten sucked into Leon Angelo's egoistic orbit.

Rabbit. Why isn't anyone contacting *me?* Why didn't anyone try harder? It's not as if people didn't know. His husband—if they're even still married—knew. Zoë *certainly* fucking knew.

Neither duck nor rabbit comes to life.

I hug my legs closer and perch my chin on my bare knees. Unsure which self-determined prophecy I'm fulfilling, I open my laptop and the video-comm program that's been the bane of my existence for several years now. The dot next to my personal icon is red. Has been for years. It takes a swig of very bad gin to gather the gumption to click that dot and turn it green.

BEEP boop BEEP boop BEEP—

Click.

Shit. I'd panicked. Closed the laptop. Another sip of something terrible, and I open it again— daintily, like I'm trying to release the tarantula I'd found in my shower back into the wild without getting attacked.

The attempted call had come from Aspen Leroy-Pierce. Or is it Aspen Leroy-Pierce-Angelo? Aspen Angelo? I never got clear on that and never cared to. Aspen was a Ph.D. student when I showed up to CNU as an M.S. transfer from the Southwest. He dropped out weeks before it came out that Leon was separating from his then-partner, Devon—and months before rumors of their engagement filtered through the department.

I just don't think my heart is really in it, Aspen had said. *And you really, really have to want it to survive a Ph.D. program.*

Funny coincidence, Leon only started wanting Aspen once Aspen stopped wanting to make a name for himself in botany.

I don't have anything against Aspen—not anymore. But I haven't even *thought* to speak with him in years. That distance combined with the half-empty bottle at my feet has not left me with much in the way of tact. So, when call attempt number two comes through, I don't bother with pleasantries and just rip off the social band-aid. "Why are you calling me?"

Aspen hesitates. The bulge of his Adam's apple shifts with his buying-for-time swallow in a way that my own throat could never imitate. Just one of many moving parts that make him the sort of man you marry. I, on the other hand, am the sort of man you bend over your desk and fuck between seminars because you're pissed at the Board of something-or-other for passing over your funding application. When I realize I've covered my throat, I let my hand fall to my lap.

Aspen says, "I heard you might be going to

the Western Expanse."

"Yeah?"

"Yeah."

"How?"

Aspen's always been unfailingly polite *and* kind. A rare combination. But losing his partner—and probably witnessing a good showing of fuck-toys at the funeral—would seem to have lowered his tolerance for niceties. "Juniper is a friend of the family," he says lightly. Makes sense. She and Leon were at Oxford together. And, having had big enough tits and big enough sense to keep her eyes on her own paper, she likely never realized what a creep Leon was—hopefully.

I fold my arms across my chest. "Okay, what of it?"

"I assume you heard what happened to Leon?"

"Death?"

Aspen gives me a ghosting smile that's hard to read on screen. "Did you hear how?"

Autoerotic asphyxiation while jacking it to every search result for FTM PUSSY GANGBANG ULTRA HARDCORE CHOKING HUMILIATION *the internet has to offer?*

"No," I say.

"Field research, by invitation of the FRF. Western Expanse." My brows shoot up at that, and Aspen continues, "He and Val Rowan left eight months ago. They were scheduled to return after four weeks."

"And neither did?"

"No," Aspen says tightly, "*Val* did. Three weeks past schedule."

"Where is she now?"

"She died after spending two weeks brain-dead at Stanford Med." Aspen looks shockingly *untroubled* by this. And this is the guy who knew the name of every student in the department, took the time to greet every secretary and janitor by name, and spent his free time volunteering at a camp for disadvantaged nerds *while* working through one of the most rigorous doctoral programs on the continent *and* working part-time at the local co-op.

"So... she was recovered?"

"After a fashion," Aspen says. "Police found her walking the highway forty miles outside the border, completely covered in dirt and blood. She lost consciousness before they even reached the hospital, so she was never questioned. They tested the blood on her; most of it was hers, but the blood beneath her fingernails—and around her mouth— that was Leon's." His posture is rigid. It's not just the overwhelming emotion, the horror of it all. He's hiding something.

No, actually. *He* isn't. That's why he's calling. Aspen has managed to stay as kind as ever—at least for some people. One of the students his partner took on as a T.A. and side-fuck barely one year into their marriage remains one of them. I ask, "What aren't they telling me?"

Aspen looks grateful for the question, like he can justify sharing now I've mustered sense enough to ask. "Before losing consciousness in the ambulance, Rowan did say one thing that wasn't just sing-songing, muttering nonsense. She said that—" He swallows again, and his words tighten. "Her *son* asked her to do it."

"Her son," I echo, narrowing my eyes.

"Her son died three years ago."

"So let me get this straight. You're telling me that Angelo and Rowan went into the Western Expanse, where Rowan's dead son told her to, what, *murder Angelo?*"

Aspen gives me an exhausted, helpless shrug. "No, Orion. I'm only telling you what *I've* been told. I don't know what happened."

"But you'd *like* to know."

"Not more than I'd like for you to tell whoever offered you this 'opportunity' to fuck themselves."

I blink at him. "Wow. I didn't know you knew that word."

"Please," Aspen says. "There is nothing to be gained by going there."

"Well, if it's any comfort, I will be going alone—"

"So did Ismene Nakamura. She's been presumed dead for years now, and she's not the first."

"I have no idea who that is."

"Entomologist, DTU."

"That'd be why."

"Look," Aspen says. "I suspect I know where this research grant originated, and if I'm right—and it's the same place Leon and Val's grant came from—you really, *really* should not be going." He takes my raised eyebrow as his cue to keep talking. "Ostensibly, the offer came through DTU, but the P.I. I hired didn't even have to dig very far to establish how flimsy that paper trail was."

"Mine isn't from DTU," I say.

Aspen leans back, surprised. "Really?"

"Yeah, it's from the President's—"

"Wife?"

"Yes…?"

"Yes," Aspen says, surprised. "That is where the trail led. You *do* know she's absolutely insane, right?"

"Well, she is married to a fascist, so I wasn't really thinking she'd make for a good emergency contact."

"She has a dozen hermetically sealed orchids at her Palm Beach palace—"

"Sounds awesome—"

"They *talk to her.*"

I sit with this information while the R2-D2-like humidifier whirs to life for its scheduled moistening activities. The thirteen-leaved *Rhynchostylis gigantea* zip-tied to a barstool hostage-style wiggles in the wet moving air. Stacked yellow-green leaves glisten to life and bounce in a flourish, like somebody's just presented the world with a budless bouquet. Most of my furniture isn't usable as furniture—actually, that's not true. It is being used as furniture, just by orchids instead of people. "Well," I say diplomatically, "I'm not really in a position to judge."

Aspen doesn't debate this last point, and he can go fuck himself about that. "Point is she has a great deal of influence, money, and power, and she is not in her right mind."

"Clearly not, if she thinks an orchid could speak loudly enough to be heard through a hermetic—"

"Do you know why her last gardener was executed?"

"Uh…" I scrunch my shoulders and offer, "Fertilizing bisexually? Gender-non-conforming watering?"

"No," Aspen says with remarkable patience, "because her favorite orchid *suggested it*. Do you know what she *calls* her favorite orchid?"

I close my eyes and sigh. "I do not, and you know that. I am way too fucking broke and tired about that for gratuitous sophistry right now, so just—"

"Her daughter," Aspen answers. "The orchid, so she claims, is her *daughter*. One of several. I don't know what happened to Leon and Val out there, or what they found. But I think this woman believes that *she* knows. And she's hoping you'll find it too— to what end, I have no clue."

I don't respond to this. He's probably right. I

just don't give a rat's ass is the thing.

"Can I share something personal with you?" Aspen asks.

"No, but I expect you're going to do it anyway." I sigh. "Yeah, sorry, sure."

"I think Leon felt threatened by you. By your talent... your insight especially."

"Oh yeah?" I scoff to cover the unpleasant prickle on my neck and shoulders.

"Yeah," Aspen echoes. "You know I asked him once where the inspiration for Elegy came from?" Aspen's sad smile wrinkles his eyes at the corners. "Fitting name for a final work, huh? Anyway, you'd think I'd ask him where he'd been last night... why he smelled like someone else's cologne." He snorts. "Like I ever bothered asking about *that*."

"You never said anything," I say blankly. A less broken version of me might have found all of this validating. All I feel is emptied. Maybe there'd been some resentment there before. Now, there's nothing. No hunger. Just the gut-deep chill the moment before the moment you realize you're about to wretch, and there's nothing there to throw up. Aspen's faint grimace seems to be expecting anger. I'm not. Guess I just wasn't raised right: to be angry. I was raised to be something else, and I am just too good at that something else for my own health.

Aspen says, "No. I didn't. I couldn't have proven it then, but... no. That's not why. I won't pretend like it is." He shrugs. "I could now though. I have access to his text messages…emails…browser history… his digital everything."

"His texts?" Leon had blocked my number. I didn't realize his devices had been able to hold onto the incriminating messages that, for me, disappeared like a rare good dream upon waking. "You read them? *All* of them?"

"All of them. And they weren't just from you." Aspen's bitter laugh doesn't suit his kind face. "Yours were far from the worst, Orion."

If the silence is as awkward for Aspen as it is for me, it doesn't show on his face. Why would it? It's not like those texts were full of *Aspen's* nudes and thirst haiku. "So… that's it?" I ask. "Your personal confession? You knew your husband had ripped off his fuck-toy?"

"Part of it… not all," Aspen admits. He breathes deeply through his nose, staring off at something I can't see. Something on the other side of his computer. "I was never going to be enough for him. But neither were you. Nobody was. He was just empty. I loved him, but he was empty. And that was the one thing he just couldn't face. Pretty weak, when you think about it."

That's no revelation to me. That it's a revelation to Aspen is something though. "*Horror vacui,*" I say, not for the first time. It is the first time I say it to somebody real, living, and there, though.

Aspen gives me a one-sided smile and translates and completes the phrase, situating it in proper ecological context. "Nature abhors a vacuum."

"Eco 101. If there is a hole, it will be filled." I wince. "Would you believe me if I said that's not what I meant?"

Aspen graces me with a worn half-smile. Amazing how he can manage just the right amount of sympathy that it doesn't seem piteous. He should teach smiling classes. Or maybe just *Human Decency 101.* "Yes, Orion. I believe you." The smile fades from his eyes. "That's why I have to ask. Why? Why risk your life for this?"

All I offer is a noncommittal shrug. He doesn't deserve the truth, but not in the way that Leon doesn't deserve to be grieved. Aspen doesn't deserve to be burdened with the knowledge of my weakness. No good can come of him learning why drowning myself milliliter by milliliter had only begun to seem so, so necessary after his husband made a habit of fingering me the one place I'd told him was off limits. He doesn't need to wonder why I kept going back for more. Why I medicated myself with alcohol to better be able to medicate myself with *him.* What I was destroying myself to hide from.

There's no need to tell him that I'm going off to war to keep from dying slowly.

Horror vacui.

Contrary to what Floridians may think, I am but a thing of nature.

And I really am no better, no stronger than Leon was.

Winter's outside but it can't reach us here. The tropical wing of the Bathurst Botanical Gardens is kept too warm for that. Massive humidifiers pump in hot, wet air that paints each pane of glass in sheets of condensation. Even at the dome's apex, that moisture doesn't freeze. Water only drips down to slide along the leaves of Painted Drop-Tongue and Vanilla. They drink it up, greedy.

I pride myself on my unflappability in the face of nature's less decorous facets, but even I've got my limits. I tug up my shirt to put as much material as possible between my nose and *that smell*. At forty-two, the corpse flower housed in the Bathurst Botanical Garden is older than me. It smells like it's been dead for roughly ninety percent of that time. Fabric filters some (but not all) of the petulance from my groan. "Why," I say, carefully flattening the vowels from my accent, "does the *smell* of something rotting hit you so much harder than just looking at it does?"

"I expect," Leon says, elegant nose barely wrinkled, "because it is with scent that we are most penetrated."

I give him a look over my rucked-up shirt. He knows what that look means. It's the facial equivalent of that editing note I keep leaving in his manuscripts: a doodled violet that means *purple prose*—often with an added hint of *pedantic*.

Leon's unbothered. "We cannot spit out a smell. It has become part of us. Dwelling in us." His smile is how I imagine a leopard might smile—if it had a mouth that could smile, for one, and knew just how magnificent that mouth looked for another.

"Julia Kristeva called," I say, insult muffled by fabric. "She wants her theory of abjection back."

I swear, the laugh that gets me could feed me for *days.*

Leon sighs; his attention returns to the reason for our visit. *A. titanum.* The corpse flower. Arguably, one of the few flowers—if not the *only* flower—that remains largely unchanged since the SMEE. It's still blooming, though its colors have dulled. Sanguine pinks and burst-capillary purples that once hinted at the exposed flesh *A. titanum* tries to mimic have faded like healed bruises. Now, there's just shades of chartreuse and watered-down jade. This drab, perpetually rotting plant is why we're here. Or that's why Leon is here. *He* is why I am here.

"Smell that?" Leon shakes his head in faint wonderment. "Amazing."

"*That's* why we're here," I say. "Not just the flower. The *smell. A. titanum* still emits an odor—and one humans can detect. You want to know why this"—I jerk my chin at the massive gray-green funnel"—and not any other flowers do so—"

"To our knowledge," Leon amends with a charitable nod.

"To our knowledge, sure. But I'm *right*." I

realize I'd hit that last vowel to sharply, too brightly, and pull my shirt a little higher up my face.

"Perhaps."

My eyes roll so hard I may actually have strained something. "*Perhaps,*" I echo under my breath. "Could be beyond the point though."

"Oh? How so?"

"Well, maybe all this means is that *A. titanum's* inflorescence, properly speaking, doesn't really qualify as a flower so much as a specialized leaf. A titanic, misshapen"—my eyes move up the massive, yellow spadix standing proud of the spathe's funnel like an obelisk—"phallic leaf."

Leon feigns disappointment with an eminently English *tsk.* "Sounds like a rather conveniently retrofitted classification to me."

"Oh, right, sorry. I forgot all good science should be *a priori.*"

"The more poetically compelling science, certainly."

My scoff earns me another of those charming smiles. I pretend to examine a nearby Mimosa pudica so he can't see just how pleased that smile's made me. He knows (and I know it), but still. It's embarrassing. I give the tiny fern-like leaves a brush of my thumb just so I don't have to be alone in the feeling. It shrivels up and curls away from my touch.

Interesting evolutionary response. Tad inefficient... melodramatic even. Still basically rational though. Now Leon's combing a stray bit of damp hair from my forehead, and I wonder why I'm not shrivelling up, curling away too. He presses his check against the side of my head and asks, "I expect you're thinking about what I'm thinking about?" His brief, silent laugh tickles my hair. "Granted, the scientific name is a *tad* on the nose."

The heaviness the conversational lull takes on tells me Leon's expecting a response. I can't give him one. I've just realized why the flower's smell hit me like a punch to the throat, triggering my mouth to water and stomach to twist—all systems readying to purge my body of death. A cat, of all things, made its way into the glass building at some point. For whatever reason, it wound up in the deep cavity of the corpse flower... must've slipped down the yellow-green folded-fan of the funneled walls, gotten wedged beneath the male flowers at the base, and died. Its fur—gray, wet, and matted—is caked in yellow pollen it was ill equipped to deliver anywhere else. There are no flies left to buzz around it, no maggots to worm their way inside. Just whatever microflora and bacterial colonies had always been there, living with that poor, lost animal. It makes for a slow, merciless decay—with a stench to match. But it can't have been more than a day. The corpse flower only blooms so long.

A squeeze on my hip bids me answer a question I can't even remember, so I do. I nod.

Leon's casual words at my temple are as good as a fist in my hair. "Then get on your knees and suck your professor's cock."

Once on the ground, the metallic *zip* of his

fly undercuts the softness of his voice. "*Such a good boy.*"

I wake up, dripping, choking on my own throat.

Knowing that Professor Leon Angelo is dead should be comforting. It should. It should keep me from clutching at my throat and abandoning my final grading to pace between the windows, checking each pane of glass for another man's reflection. It doesn't.

He feels closer, now that he's dead.

After waking up at noon followed by six hours of being completely ineffectual, I do what everyone probably knew I was going to do anyway and give all my students A's. That deserves a celebration. Celebrations deserve alcohol. I'm halfway through one bottle of distilled celebration and my ultra-specific orchid-care guide when my front door opens to a Polynesian woman and a piercing New Mexico sunset. Both briefly set the foliage in my apartment ablaze. Rae closes the door behind her, and all is green again. Quick arithmetic follows the observation that her braided black hair is streaked with gray. I haven't seen her in almost six years. The rest of her is largely unchanged: still tall, still chubby, still rocking the oversized off-the-shoulder shirt over a slutty lace bustier look. If I'd been smarter in undergrad, I'd have been chasing after her. But I wasn't, so here we are: single, abusing several substances, and hoarding orchids.

"This isn't Vancouver," I say, stupidly.

Rae also finds this stupid. Her face says so and everything. Concerned I'm too dumb to clock that too, she adds, "What a stupid thing to say to me"—just in case. It's fine. Directness is blunted when dealt in a New Zealand accent.

Rae doesn't bother asking for permission before taking off her boots and sauntering, tote bag clinking into the kitchen for a cabinet deep-dive. "Where do you keep the—" She pulls out a wine glass I haven't bothered with since moving to New Mexico. I'm kind of amazed it doesn't have an orchid in it. Rae snorts, says, "Shocked it doesn't have an orchid in it," then draws a bottle of wine far classier than anything I'd have bought myself from her tote bag, and pours herself a glass.

"Yeah... must've forgot it was there." I go back to honing my ultra-specific orchid-care guide notes.

"That checks out." She leans against the counter, one hand resting on her waist, the other swirling her glass. Gold bangles on her wrist *clink* with every motion like she's cheers-ing herself. She'd have to. I only have the one wine glass.

"So..." I venture, "what's up?"

Rae sucks her teeth and shakes her head, muttering to herself. I catch "This guy," and that's it.

If Aspen knows about my trip, then of course Rae (his former office mate and current fellow journal editor), would know. And if Rae knows, so does her cousin. That fleeting conceptual contact with my ex is enough to make me bury myself back in orchid-sitting instructions in the hopes Rae will take the hint and leave.

She doesn't—just takes in the empty take-out cartons overflowing from the recycling bin, and the many plants around her. "So... you're leaving tomorrow then?"

"Yup."

"Have you even *started* packing yet?"

My mouth makes a vaguely affirmative noise, but the rest of me is carefully scribbling in an addendum to the "*Epidendrum porpax* (bathroom cabinet)" section. I clock her glare and ask, "What *does* one pack for a twelve-week trip to a climatologically inscrutable and politically nefarious destination?" Rae keeps glaring. "You're thinking *layers*, huh?" I sigh. "Fine. I'll pack now. Happy?"

Rae downs her wine and follows me into the bedroom, unhappy.

"I'm guessing you're here to convince me *not* to go?"

"I think you should probably do the opposite of whatever it is you've decided to do, and I'd wager you've decided not to..." Rae's brow pinches as she watches me dig out a duffel bag, plop it onto my unmade bed, and begin wantonly tossing underwear inside. "Oh!"

"Seriously? You thought I'd turn down a fully funded research trip to the swamps of *Florida?*

International capital of trans rights and shining beacon of racial harmony?"

"Well, I'd rather *hoped*, yes!" Rae's face is oddly impressed. As if she hadn't realized just how far my self-destructive streak was capable of streaking, and now she's watching it tear off all its clothes and run laps through the Santa Fe Plaza during the lunch rush at peak tourist season.

"Well, your mistake."

"You're not going."

"Cute," I say, tossing socks into my duffel bag like a footnote that reads: *Eat my entire dick.* She knows it, too. I pause, staring meaningfully at a water stain on the wall before considering my shirt choices thus far. "*Is* Florida still a swamp? We clear on that yet?"

Rae shrugs, staring into her wine glass. She gives it a swirl that splashes a blush of red light onto her chin and cheeks. Carefully minding the orchid growing out of a Chinese take-out container, she places her glass on the dresser with a soft *tink*. Then she doesn't say anything. This lasts a respectable (for her) fifteen seconds before she's striding forward, pulling clothes out of my bag and refolding them to her Virgo-standards. "You're too fucking *gay* to be so bad at this."

"I'm breaking down barriers and crushing stereotypes. What have *you* done for the community lately?"

"*Adorable.*"

"Hold on," I say. "I only just talked to Aspen

yesterday. You can't have gotten the time off on such short notice. You were already coming here. Why?"

Rae's lips disappear. She was never that great of a liar, and her existence gives the cliché that alcohol is a truth potion most of its credence.

I let out a ragged sigh that makes me feel about two inches shorter. "Just tell me."

"It can wait, really, and—"

"Rae."

Rae's eyes move to the old cowboy hat on my dresser and the *Epidendrum porpax* holed up inside, its roots hugging a dried strip of bark I'd found in the desert. The hat was an impulse buy made during a road trip through San Jose. Rae was there. Her cousin, too. So was a version of me that didn't not wear certain hats or shoes or shirts because somebody else didn't like them. That hat was beat up long before I got to it, so she can't blame the wear on its being repurposed as a vivarium. Leather I can only imagine used to be black is faded gray now. It's as covered in creases and bruises and wrinkles as anybody lucky enough to do a lot of living. Makes it comfortable. Pale, silvery lines run along the underside of its wide brim in places, soft and subtle as veins seen through brown skin.

The orchid it's hosting is small, but big enough that it would have been flowering by now— if it lived in times gentler than these. Matte green, ochre-tipped stalks once designed to hold sunrise blossoms just curl at the tips, ending nowhere but themselves. Rae gentles some roots aside—maybe trying to determine if my hat's ever going to be wearable again, or if it's just been irredeemably parasitized. "I didn't want you to find out on your own. Or...." She doesn't finish, but her intent is clear enough: she didn't want me to *be* alone when I found out.

I don't bother asking again. Rae stops folding underwear, clasps her hands together and closes her eyes. "Zoë's going on maternity leave next year. She's due in July. Twins."

"Neat," says the man standing on my floor and wearing my clothes and speaking my words and packing my clothes while I watch from anywhere else. I continue selecting suitable socks from the laundry hamper. Nobody could possibly need as many socks as I've already tossed into that duffel, but I do not care.

"Yeah," Rae admits with a sad smile. "She seems very happy."

"That's real swell—*fuck!*" The sudden sting brings me back to myself5, and myself just got his finger sliced by a broken bit of plastic and is bleeding all over my (formerly) clean clothes.

"Oh no, Orion, sweetheart, let me—"

"I got it," I say. "It's not deep." It might be, I don't know. I'm compressing it with a sock far too tightly to find out, and I don't mean to find out so long as Rae's still here, still looking at me like I'm liable to try my hand at self-lobotomization next.

Her voice is quiet as a pulse when she says, "Zöe still ca—"

"We really don't have to talk about—"

"What happened was *tragic*—"

"No," I cut in. "It wasn't tragic. See, tragedy implies fate. A lack of agency. *She* had choices and she picked one of them. She *chose* to not only *reject* her best friend and partner after he transitioned, but then she chose lie to him for fucking months about her *new* partner—a *real* man, because it turns out men are fine when they're *born with dicks*—before fucking off and changing her fucking number instead of having a tough conversation—"

"I know," Rae soothes. "I didn't mean tragic in the technical sense." Under her breath, she adds, "Fucking pedant."

I toss my blood-soaked sock in the vicinity of the hamper with a blank *"Touché."*

Silence rolls in. Rae rolls out. Unlike her cousin, *she* comes back—with first-aid supplies I didn't know I had. After sterilizing and bandaging my cut, she asks, "Feel better?"

I consider my wanton pyramid of socks. The pyramidion breaks ranks and tumbles to the floor. I mumble, *"No,"* eyes still fixed on those rogue, red socks. Red and purple, actually. Not even a matching pair.

"You won't find it," Rae says.

"The other red sock?"

"The orchid, you absolute numpty."

I'm more shocked than anybody to realize I'm not lying when I say, "I *could* though."

"You won't."

"But I *could*."

"Sure, theoretically, yes, I suppose there is a minuscule—dare I say statistically insignificant—possibility that you could find it, you are correct. *Technically*."

"Exactly." At her utterly perplexed look, I ask, "How could I know that and *not try?*" I laugh at myself. Just about those same words got said when I finally voiced my desires and doubts aloud: if I should accept the risk, the effort, the cost of transitioning. 'How could you know it *might* make you happy and not *try?*' she'd asked me, before I knew just how insane hope really is. I'm too tired, to empty to be properly insane.

"You should wear the cowboy hat."

"Pardon?"

"You should," Rae says. "You look handsome in it, and they did used to call Florida the sunshine state, didn't they?"

"Maybe ironically?"

"Look. Sweetie." Rae takes my hands in hers and gives them a gentle squeeze, careful to avoid the bandaged finger. It's the first gentle, casual touch I've experienced in a long time. Either that recognition, or the touch itself—maybe both—hits me like a slap. Rae holds me tighter. "Come visit me some time," she pleads with the tone of a woman trying to get a toddler to eat something *green* for once. "There are people doing some really incredible stuff with synthetic semiochemicals. Personal interests aside, Bathurst is probably *the place* for you to be." She does her best not to let too much of her frustration show on her face. "At least *visit*. For *me*."

I won't. She doesn't need to know why. Maybe I'll tell her one day.

When the dead stop feeling so, *so* much more alive than me.

Undergoing a physical evaluation is routine for these sorts of visa applications—especially ones involving field work. I already have my FRF visa. This physical was ordered by my own department, and I've only got a few hours between my appointment and my train. It's entirely my own fault. In my defense, I fucking hate doctors. After two decades of lost civil rights progress, trans people once again belong to a protected class—*theoretically*. Medical discrimination, *legally* speaking, is once again a thing of the past—*theoretically*. But, as anybody with a Ph.D. on a crashing plane can tell you: theory is pretty fucking useless.

"How many weeks since your last period?" the nurse asks—again.

"Don't know," I say flatly. "What year is it?"

She frowns at her tablet. "Oh! You had a hysterectomy? That's not on your chart."

"No, I have not had one. Does that disqualify me from field research?"

No acknowledgment. She just pushes the paper gown off my shoulders with one hand, wrangling a stethoscope onto her ears with the other. Her eyes give the gingko branch tattooed across my collarbone a passing glance. Now, they are fixed on my bare chest as she places the cold steel disk onto my sternum. I'm 90% sure she's not actually listening for anything.

"Oh, hm…" she muses, "suppose it's still hard to find a good transgender surgeon." She pinches the puckered flesh bulging from either side of my ribs for no medical reason whatsoever and adds, "You're gonna need another surgery to fix that, huh. But you're still not done yet anyway, so that's okay."

"Wow," I say, staring at the hand fondling the faint scars crossing my chest. "All that really just got said out loud, huh?"

This too, shockingly enough, receives no acknowledgment. "My niece is transgendered," she confides with the air of someone admitting to giving the homeless person they see on their daily commute a five-dollar Dunkin gift card at Christmas time. "She wants to get a mastectomy too, but her mom was telling me that a lot of doctors are still nervous about specializing in those things. But you can still get a hysterectomy!" She says this last bit with an encouraging smile.

Good heavens, if I did that, what man would fuck me? Sheer exhaustion is the only thing keeping this thought from leaping out my no-fucks-to-spare mouth and punching her in the throat.

"You know," she goes on, "I did hear there's a

great doctor in Mexico—"

"Sure, I'll get right on that. Getting my genitalia sliced and diced in a foreign land definitely tops my priority list"—I glance at her name tag so I know whom to thank in my bedtime prayers—"*Kayleigh.*"

After that, the three-hour train ride to Texas is a glorious respite and takes hardly any time at all. The bar car did help. The train to Florida, which has no bar car and a dozen security stops, takes roughly sixteen years. Any alleged hangovers and nurse-induced tension headaches only get partial blame for the temporal dilation. Most goes to the fascist police state.

Getting visa access to the FRF should have taken months. Even years. But the President's wife has been dreaming of orchids and pulling strings to make them bloom. My visa arrived (according to my passport) two months before the drone dropped it off last week.

THE FREE REPUBLIC OF FLORIDA

NAME: Orion Rael Armijo
BIOLOGICAL SEX: Male
DATE OF BIRTH: Sep 27 2029
AFFILIATION: University of Atalaya (New Mexico)
PURPOSE OF VISIT: Research
LENGTH OF STAY: 12 weeks

My twenty-eight-year-old face stares back at me from the digital card: hair black, skin smooth and the deep gray of winter bark. The dark stubble I have now was nothing but a wish and a prayer for him. Maybe Past-Me had made a bargain. My kingdom for a horse! My sense of place in the universe for some manly stubble!

The few women I've dated tell me it scratches their lips.

The men who fuck me ask me to shave it off before I suck their dick.

How else is a guy supposed to self-medicate when the problem is consciousness? At least, consciousness is the problem most easily remedied. Maybe there'd been gentler medicines before. Teas brewed from meadows, subtle and sweet. Chamomile was one. Lavender another. Lavender does still exist. It's a colorless grass nearly the exact shade of gray as twenty-eight-year-old Me's cheeks. The stalks smell a bit like soap, if you stretch your imagination—like grass but more sterile somehow. Neither scientists nor homeopaths can identify any trace of something like a psychotropic effect. The plant makes no attempt to act on anyone beyond itself.

Chamomile is gone, though. Like so many flowers, it couldn't adapt to the loss of its pollinators. Artificial means never seemed to cut it for long, either. It's one of Ishida's Ninety: those plants that, for reasons completely mysterious to us, could not be pollinated via drone without— seemingly spontaneously—dying. Rotting away from the roots. As if their whole existence recoiled at the very notion of being pollinated, touched, by something artificial and not biological.

Like most people I've slept with: *It's not the same! I hate the feel of silicone; I don't care how indistinguishable it's been proven to be in blind tests! Wouldn't it be easier if I just fucked you? The possibility of you coming in my nostril when I give you head is important to me, spiritually!*

Or something. Fuck, my brain is really on a roll today. The trouble with being smart is I'm perfectly aware that these mental spirals are just as much self-medication as cough syrup and vodka. Positive affirmations don't work (except maybe for the sort of people who don't need to self-medicate in the first place). If you really want to keep your mind from dwelling where it really hurts, stop tonguing the wound that's still festering, still pulsing, still liable to burst open and make your whole existence go septic, you need to pace in a *neighboring* mental room that only stings about 70% as deeply.

Fortunately, knowing this doesn't make it less effective. The human mind is an absolute fucking trip.

The train slows to welcome yet another wave of black-uniformed border patrol agents, each armed to the teeth with guns, tasers, and entitlement. A white man with a sweat-shined neck and cropped blonde hair asks me for my passport, shoving out one black-gloved hand. The other remains on his hip holster. I hadn't bothered putting my passport away after the last stop twenty minutes ago.

Clever me.

"Research," the man reads, closely set blue eyes moving over the document. "Research where?"

I answer, "The Western Expanse," and the officer (plus two more, also blonde) stare right at me, dead silent. They're giving overgrown Children of the Corn meets the SS vibes. It's hard to focus on anything but how badly I wish I had something to drink. My throat sounds about as good as it feels, and it sounds *rough*—which does make my voice deeper, so that's something. I clear my throat and add, "I'm an"—figuring they probably don't have 'ecologists' in Florida, I go with—"natural philosopher."

The officer nods. His eyes go back to the passport, searching out any irregularity—anything worth questioning. Nothing. He nods and passes my passport back to me. "Welcome to the Free Republic of Florida, Mr. Armijo," pronouncing my name like he's auditioning for the role of *racist jackboot #4* and leaving nothing on the field.

I'm too train- and fuckboy-weary *not* to correct him. I straighten my cowboy hat and lie, "It's *Doctor,* Army Joe."

After passing the last of the walls between me and the Western Expanse, there is a trail to follow... until there isn't. Odd thing is, there's not a total lack of visible trails so much as an overabundance of them. The wilderness here doesn't really feel wild. It feels manicured. Like somebody's been coming in here and raking up all the fallen leaves, pulling up any weeds before they could take root and spoil all that nice blank space between the trees.

It's quiet. Even my footsteps are quiet on this neatly combed ground that I hesitate to even call "earth." The silence buzzes, agitating me.

This place bears all the stillness of a deep winter's night.

Only, it's midday.

And May.

The map they gave me—an honest to goodness laminated physical map—isn't terribly informative, which makes the compass they also gave me—an honest to goodness magnet and needle on a little dial—similarly useless. There are precious few landmarks to speak of. But as I go farther and farther west, I start to realize something. The border patrolled by guards with guns isn't really the border. I don't think I'm in the Western Expanse yet. Something about the way it's getting harder and harder to make out the space between trees in the far distance, like they've been painted over with fog, tells me I'm going to be there soon.

Nothing else tells me shit.

I check the map again. No indication of any neighborhoods. No mention of anything manmade *at all*. How did this map even *come to exist?* Had they just taken an old map, pasted a field of red over the no-go zone, and erased everything inside but a vague idea of where bodies of water might be?

The Western Expanse is hundreds of miles across, spanning what used to be Tallahassee halfway up to Montgomery and stretching into Louisiana. Some of those places were major population centers before the SMEE—weren't they? I was born in the western Republic of Texas, but I moved to New Mexico to live with my grandmother in middle school. After that, I did my best to never move farther east than my grandma's driveway if I could help it—and I only went that far because of filial obligation (and the best carne adovada in town). But I'm pretty sure there used to be a lot of people in those areas. Said people were a big factor in keeping *me out* of those places. Come to the Free Republic of Florida for the bigotry, stay for the humidity.

I wipe my forehead with my sleeve, dab at my cheeks. I'm not hot. I'm condensating. It's so humid, I'm collecting dew like the windshields that—maybe, maybe not—used to be here. The trees aren't closer together than they were. And yet, they are. It's the other plants. That's what's different now. It isn't just trees, its shrubs and vines and weeds and ferns and budless flowers. I have to stop and just stare at it all—I haven't seen this much biodiversity in the wild outside of documentary footage since I was a little kid. My sleeve's already damp from environmental moisture, but I use it to wipe at my cheeks again anyway then keep walking—always due west.

Something admittedly unscientific makes me think this stretch of wilderness I'm treading through now might just be one of those recently populated places. It isn't an intuition. It's a physical feeling. There's a hollow stiffness far, far beneath my feet, buried beneath several feet of loam and dirt. It feels like treading over freshly dug graves.

Thousands of them.

Fog hangs heavy in the cold, knit between the trees. At first, I don't even recognize that distant flash of silver for what it is: something inorganic. Something people left behind. An antique airstream trailer.

When I was eleven, I was sent to live with my grandmother on the border between Texas and New Mexico—on the New Mexico side, thankfully. Her house was small, but her property was a huge sprawl of desert, rocks, and juniper. A tiny boat bobbing on a boundless sea, always in danger of getting swallowed up (and Grandma didn't seem to be fighting that too hard). Brambles, vines, cacti, all sorts of shrubs encroached on the house, growing into the walls. Once, chamisa even poked its way into the kitchen, tunneling its way in beneath the door. Must have followed the tarantulas and scorpions inside.

This trailer park reminds me of that. But without a friendless teenager desperate for distraction to prune back the worst of the weeds. It's also in northwestern Florida, so it isn't just the plants and animals that eat away at homes. It's the air.

Four trailers have been left behind. From the tree line, I count four empty foundations, and four more spots I can only guess stood beneath mobile homes. The thicker, hardier vines support the smaller ones, hoisting them up to places they couldn't have reached otherwise. One mobile home is tilted on its wheels, pulled back by vines. It's like watching a sea monster drag a ship down into the depths in ultra slow motion. In a few decades, maybe, that mobile home will be bones beneath the earth.

Had Angelo and the others found this place? Or am I just very, very bad at compasses? I give the thing a little shake. The needle falters only to settle in a different direction entirely. It both is and isn't a comfort that it's not me who's bad at compasses. *Florida* is bad at compasses. That, or they gave me a shit one on purpose. Maybe as a joke. Border guards have to get their jollies somehow.

I really ought to be looking for signs of the other scientists' presence, but that's not what I find myself doing. I'm no archaeologist, but I can't help trying to suss out a timeline for this trailer park. Cars would have been useful to that end, but there are none. Maybe the inhabitants all fled by car before the area was cordoned off—if there ever were any. I don't even see a road. Did it already melt away into the earth?

The green surrounding me takes on a deeper, cooler tone. It'll be dark soon. Maybe I shouldn't be wasting time here before I've located Waypoint Four and set up camp. But if whatever happened to Angelo and Rowan had something to do with the environment, maybe I *should* be setting up camp anywhere else. In which case, the total lack of evidence of their presence might actually be a stroke of good luck for once.

I wonder if there's any liquor stashed in one of these trailers.... In a flash, it occurs to me: I'm one day sober. Does contrived sobriety count?

A discolored beige-vinyl-sided trailer stands out to me. It's been sealed shut by rust even as that same rust opens windows along its ribs, the holes expanding, joining. Ovals of corrosion consolidate into cumulus cloud shapes that outline the darkness within. At my push, the door opens two inches. I need to find a crowbar or something to get inside, but my eyes won't budge from the holes the air has eaten into the walls. Dozens of mouths hang open in a permanent scream—at what's inside? Or outside?

I shrug out of my pack and grab a plank to find out.

First thing I find out is that there's a sharp band of aluminum wedged in the wood.

"Fuck me!"

Thin blood's already running so fast from my hand to my elbow, I can't make out where the cut actually is. The navy bandana in my left pocket is sacrificed at the altar of my stupidity. I wrap it around my wrist and force my way inside, propelled by spite.

The musty wet smells of outside are concentrated in here, but there's a sharp edge to it. Household cleaners? Some ghosting artifact of human presence? Woody vines have colonized the living room, surrounding cradling the TV and making themselves comfortable inside the sofa cushions. Not much blocks my way to the kitchen but dried leaf litter on the linoleum.

The first cabinet I check is soggy. The door breaks apart at my touch, exposing stacked and mismatched Tupperware. The next is stocked with clouded jars of homemade preserves. Most of the lids are bulbous, the metal straining at gasses expelled by molds that have been gorging themselves on peach jam and hot pepper jelly for years.

The biggest jar is unlabeled, filled halfway with crystal-clear liquid. I make clumsy work of the lid. One sniff tells me that it's either moonshine or acetone: either way, it's antiseptic. This is confirmed when pouring it on feels like Satan just pissed on my tender insides. Now I can see the cut. It's not as bad as the blood made it look—just nicked some capillaries. Another slosh of liquor and/or nail polish remover sterilizes my bandana compress. There's an emergency med kit in my pack, but this is faster.

Pouring liquor all over myself and the floor

also keeps me from drinking it. That's just efficiency. I huff a wry laugh. Guess my sobriety isn't contrived anymore. That might even feel pretty good if not for, well... everything else. I frown at the blue fabric concealing my second stupidity-induced injury that week.

Embarrassing.

The stale, moldy smells and black dots peppering the ceilings of every trailer have me setting up camp outside. My red, lantern-illuminated tent stands in the center of the trailer park like a campfire surrounded by covered wagons. Almost cozy. No way I'm sleeping, though.

Blood-stained bandana wrapped tightly around my face, I go back to exploring trailers. One, guarded by moss-covered garden gnomes, doesn't have a door. Maybe it never did; the interior just feels welcoming—all cherry gingham, smiling rabbit figurines, and faux-wicker furniture. The walls are covered in nothing but mold, creeping vines, and pictures of loved one. So is the pink fridge.

Water damage has glued the photos together into an inexorable collage. On the bottom, a take-away menu for a burger joint called *Harry's Roadhouse* hangs on like an artificial limb. Its once glossy flying pig logo is veiled in deep turquoise mold. I pull out my pocket microscope and hold my breath. Winking, I zoom in on the menu. The pig's pink body is composed of tiny red, yellow, and white dots. Blotches of deep blue and green are chomping away at it, starting from the legs and wings.

I take two steps back and let myself breathe again. Say what you will about New Mexico, at least I don't have to contend with water damage. Desiccation is a bitch on archives, sure, but water damage is an absolute cunt.

My brain is still itching. My body still feels the weight of my pack it hasn't even been carrying for hours now. By the time it's dark enough that I can't make out anything beyond my tent but stars, little shocks start buzzing in my head like somebody's stabbing tiny cattle prods into the back of eyeballs. Shuteye seems like the best option. I undress down to my underwear and settle into my sleeping bag, berating myself for pouring out that liquor. Hangover headaches aren't fun, but withdrawal ones are the water damage of headaches.

My eyes pulse open to complete darkness. I can't have been asleep more than an hour—headache must have woken me up. That, or the crawling sensation on my chest. It's not so unusual. Since my top surgery six years ago, I hardly ever feel my chest at all anymore except for the odd phantom sensation. If not that, *pain.* Before surgery, I didn't touch my chest if I could help it—even averted my gaze when showering. During recovery, though, I got into the habit of patting along my chest with my hands to remind myself it was still there, that the part of me containing my heart and lungs still existed. It's an odd thing, touching yourself without feeling yourself being touched. For those weeks before the stitches holding my cut-down and relocated nipple grafts in place were removed, the stiff strings felt like eyes blinking against my palms. Eyes that weren't a part of me.

When these strange sensations don't pass as usual, I gather the wherewithal to exhume my hand from beneath my side and place a hand to my chest how I've done so many times. It isn't nylon lashes blinking against my palm.

It's a tongue, licking it.

Something soft but firm and very much there *wriggles* beneath my fingers. Something *alive*. Forcing myself to stay calm, I clasp my fingers around it as gently as I can so I can identify it without squishing it while searching out my lantern. I pat around for it with my other hand. I feel my knife, my shoes. My notebook means my lantern should be right there. It is. But the switch squishes against my fingers. I brush whatever it is away, suddenly far less concerned about squishing the specimen cradled against my chest.

Light fills the tent. The floor is swarming with fat, wriggling maggots. They've completely covered the bandana I left crumpled beside me, sucking the blood off of it. They're inside my shoes. All over my sleeping bag—*inside* my sleeping bag. I look down and see red.

The maggots aren't just on my chest. They're

feeding from it. Gnawing the dead flesh down to red, still-beating tissue. The nipples a surgeon had sliced away, cut up and stitched back on are half devoured already. Each one has attracted a ring of maggots, all fighting for access to that dead skin like too many piglets fighting for purchase on a sow. They've already exposed two crescent moons of tender pink, glistening and raw like a burn.

"No, no, no," I mutter over and over, flicking the maggots from my chest with shaking hands. With each shift and move I make to get out of my sleeping bag, maggots burst open beneath my weight. Their spilled insides make me slip more than once. The heaviest thing I can reach is my lantern. Using the flat base, I smash every maggot I can find, leaving behind deflated pale-flesh balloons. Only the ones I've swept off my chest bleed.

I scramble outside, lantern in hand, shaking out maggots from my boots before slipping them on and stomping those too. Maggots means insects. Flies. Precious, presumed extinct pollinators. Rationally, I should be mortified at all this carnage. But staring down at the flattened, soured-milk pink bugs, all I feel is the lingering tickle of their feeding mouths along my shoulders and neck. I check my chest, fingers combing over my skin again and again.

Nothing there but scars, and the nipples that are basically scars themselves.

I look down. Thin rusty smears of dried

blood, dark brown freckles, sparse black hair, and two nipples, both whole and intact, still where the surgeon had stitched them in place—just a little too close to center to look anything but odd. On the ground, the flattened bodies of a dozen maggots are still there. One of them, only half squished, is still wriggling toward me—toward the smell of blood. I watch it a moment before giving it a quick, merciful stomp.

My ragged pants come out in clouds of vapor. It's freezing. Something I've only realized once free of parasites. "Fuck," I breathe out, looking out at the faint glow of pink edging the eastern horizon. The west is still a thick, inky indigo, but I can make out the trees now. Longleaf pines emerge from gold grasses and green fronds in perfect rows, each one just shy of my own hugging arms in diameter, each the same four-story height. These lucky specimens outlived the local timber industry. But the shape that industry left behind is unmistakable, however many shrubs grow in between.

Staring into the woods, the perspective is almost too perfect. It reminds me of a drawing I might've done in art class to practice vanishing points as a kid. With a step to the left, all the trees shift as one. The patches of faint violet sky beyond and between shift in time with them. It's like sitting in a room at night with half-closed blinds on the windows, and as a car drives past those bars are cast in light along the wall, moving and expanding in perfect proportion. I take another step to the left, just to watch the bars move again.

An older tree, far bigger than the rest, stands out amidst its cultivated cousins. Rough patchwork bark peels back in places. Some of those patches are a smooth, faint sienna, others a dark wrinkled gray. At first glance, I think the siena pieces are actually exposed wood, but no. It's all bark.

Something's moving in the trees. I go still, all too aware that I'm basically naked. Rustling leaves. Shifting grass. The snap of a branch that wouldn't bend. A deep, rumbling, cough of a sound. More snapping twigs. Another bass-deep cough. Something alive and much bigger than me *whines* with a voice far deeper than my own.

Not taking my eyes of the source, I turn off my lantern. Dawn is barely approaching, but there's enough light that the forest comes into focus. A black shape disrupts the vertical pattern of trees.

Someone is standing behind the oldest and thickest of the pines. More than half of their silhouette is concealed by the tree, but it's clear they are tall and broad.

My knife is still in the tent. I run through possibilities to what—or whom—that silhouette belongs. There shouldn't be much in the way of predators out here, not since being starved of their prey. But then, I didn't think I'd be seeing maggots, either.

And there are a dozen apex predators on this continent far, far less rare than flies.

A crackling groan rumbles beyond the trees.

It's getting closer now.

With a slow, shallow breath, I turn on my lantern—then freeze.

It's a black bear. Male. Standing six feet tall, leaning against a tree that creaks under his weight. Light catches the vapor cloud of his breath, haloing his sunken face and lighting up the white blaze on his chest in pale blue. He collapses to all fours, not even looking at me as he trots a few steps closer.

This animal will be younger than the SMEE. Younger than whatever cataclysm drove the Florida government to cordon off hundreds of square miles from the rest of the world, including themselves. He doesn't know that humans are to be tagged along after, but from a distance. Warily. Humans are sources of scavengeable food, but prone to violence. Often accompanied by mass mechanical means of death and destruction. Distressing sounds. Unpleasant smells.

In better circumstances, a bear that size should weigh five hundred pounds, minimum. I'd say this one can barely push three hundred pounds wet. I don't think he's even noticed me. His gaze is fixed on a spot on the ground. He limps toward whatever it is. I spot the red thing once he begins nuzzling it. A book. My sweat is freezing now, but all my attention is on that bear, and watching him try to feed from that book.

The bear pins it down with one paw, but still struggles to get a good bite. He's missing teeth. He's missing *most* of his teeth. The next growling breath doesn't even emit a cloud of vapor. It's not because the air's gotten warmer; I can still see my own breaths.

The bear's face goes down before his front limbs do. He holds himself there for ten seconds before gravity takes over and he falls with a hollow thud, landing in a tangle of papery vines and roots.

With far less caution than is merited, I move closer. His side deflates under my gaze—suddenly, like I've just stomped on his ribs. The last breath pushed out of him wheezes and groans like faulty ventilation equipment; it smells like this creature's been dead and decomposing for months now. I kneel down on bare knees and place my hand against a chapped gray paw pad. Not even warm. But then, my hands aren't warm either.

What do you say to a dead bear that's fallen when you are alone in the woods? *Sorry?* Maybe. Death means nothing to a forest. The passing of any individual is as real as that individual species' Latin name. I frown, trying to recall his. Ursus something. *Americanus?* Or did Florida's state scientists change it? *Ursus Floridanus* maybe.

Doesn't matter. Not to anyone here.

Even as I think that, my hand moves to the bear's head to rest on thinning black fur. There's no harm in touching the starved. It could have been an infection or parasite that dealt the killing blow, but it probably couldn't have if the bear had been decently nourished. Maybe I'll get lucky and contract fleas from this brief contact. Hell, I'd be halfway to claiming a Nobel Prize. Might make up for the mass murder of flies.

I lightly pinch and stroke the bear's thin, pink ear—how my grandma's dog used to like. It's already gone cold. Still soft, though.

I don't know much about the state of the Western Expanse ecosystem, clearly. But if it's anything like the rest of the continent, there won't be much left to the necrobiome. Not now that this bear is dead. Maybe some coyotes are still fucking around, but no scavenging birds or rodents or insects will come. And when I go back to my tent, I won't find any trace of maggots. I know that. My only comfort is knowing the source of such lifelike hallucinations probably wasn't whatever drove Val Rowan mad. It's just chemistry. Barely two days sober, and I'm already detoxing.

Hard truth is, nothing bigger than a few cells will aid in returning this beast to the forest that bore it. Who knows how long it will take before this flesh is available to the nest of roots cradling his body in death? I grab the torn, wrinkled book, get up, and leave the bacteria to their slow, lonely work.

Sure enough, there is no trace of maggots in the tent—just the mess I made fighting off all those tiny, wriggling windmills. Even so, I can't bring myself to linger inside. After getting dressed, I sit on some rotting wooden steps leading up to a half-eaten trailer and study the ragged book by the light of sunrise. That bear could barely get a bite in, but this book hasn't escaped the food chain. Most of it's been eaten away by mold—which might just be the new apex predator of these woods.

The wrinkled, red softcover book looks like a research journal, but it isn't. There are no field observations, no log of data entries. Each squared page is a letter to someone. Some are just a few sentences, most several paragraphs. One in the beginning approaches short-story length—not that I can read it. Rain has made a watercolor self-portrait of most of the surviving pages. Washed-out blues and grays from two different colored inks blend into stormy clouds that span page to page. The middle pages, though, have remained the most legible. One dated December 11 reads:

Hiya, Beautiful...

It's stiflingly hot. I'm starting to think I'm not in the Northern Hemisphere anymore. It is the (ostensibly) Free Republic of Florida... so maybe this country's climate's just gone as topsy-turvy as its people? Madness must be catching. Seems like every time I turn around, I find out Angelo's been putting on more layers.

No wonder Aspen asked me to keep an eye on him. And here I was, thinking the poor kid was worried about Floridian twinks making a play for his husband. That was uncharitable of me. Aspen was right to be worried. (God help me, I could hear you tsk-ing at me!)

Please permit me one last uncharitable thought—on account of it being so dismally hot and sticky out here.

What kind of pretentious asshat do you have to be to still insist on writing with a fountain pen in uncharted wilderness? What's he going to use when he spills his bottle of ink? Blood? No doubt he'd find that poetic.

That may have been three uncharitable thoughts rolled into one.

In my defense, it's VERY muggy. I swear, this air's so thick it makes a sound. Sometimes I really do think I can hear it... something in the air.

(Maybe somebody should have been sent to chaperone me)

I love you, I love you, I love you.
We will be together again soon.
I think of you often, and miss you always.
We WILL GET THROUGH THIS!
Yours (from there and back again),
V

I turn through the stiff, water-warped pages for any useful information. There are several mentions of Waypoint Four, increasingly disparaging references to Leon, complaints about how hot the weather is, how loud the starlings are?

"What the fuck..." I mouth, flipping through a mess of stains both ink and organic. The words get bigger and bigger until only a dozen fit on a page:

MOMMY LOVES YOU SO, SO MUCH
MOMMY KNOWS IT HURTS
YOU'RE SUCH A GOOD BOY

I don't know that Val Rowan made it all the way over here, but she may have. Either way, there's a good chance she covered the ground between where her journal ended up and Waypoint Four. Waypoint Four, at least, is marked on the map. If I am where I think I am, all I need to do is keep the cypress swamp on my right until I reach it.

The way the splayed, fluted roots of the cypress disappear so suddenly beneath flat water makes it look like they're all balanced on glass. Oil-slick standing water glimmers in a rainbow that shifts with each step I take. The surface is totally still. Mirror like. In old movies, the characters would be smacking at their own necks and arms to kill the mosquitos hounding them—the mosquitos that weren't would be dancing ripples across the water's surface.

Motion catches my eye. A large ripple forms several yards away from me. I squint at it, but can't make out a cause. All I see is the shining tip of a root pointing at the water as if to say, "Here it is... come see."

But there is nothing to see.

I keep moving through six more miles of *nothing to see.*

By mile seven, I'm not even consulting the map or compass anymore so much as letting my feet follow the contours of the forest. Thick roots, the precise shade of the dirt, run beneath my feet like a corduroy road made the wrong way.

These roots aren't tree roots, so what are they?

Each attempt to trace them somewhere ends in frustration. Just when I think I've made sense of them, they disappear underground or beneath a silent, unmoving bog. At first, following the roots was a way of passing the time, but now that I've seen them perfectly mimic cypress bark before disappearing beneath a cypress tree, they become much more. I start to jog in search of their next appearance.

The roots reemerge from the dirt another forty paces away, but not just anywhere. It takes a few moments to identify just what I'm seeing: roots and earth so thoroughly embedded and entangled, they look like pottery guided by hand from a single, spinning wheel of fawn-gray clay. And that dusty clay has been molded into the form of a coyote. From its curled-up position, one might've mistaken it for a sculpture of a sleeping dog. Something beloved. But the exposed jaw, rib bones discernible from spine to tip, and sunken, empty eyes break the illusion.

This thing is dead—long dead. That, or these roots are in the habit of imitating dead animals in addition to their neighbor plants. MicroRNA can be exchanged between host and parasite. Even a microbe can guide the gene expression of plants, convince it to turn purple or green or spiky or short.

But outside sea slugs, I've never encountered that level of post-transcriptional manipulation or adaptation between plant and animal species.

I kneel down for a closer look, letting my fingertips hover over the contours. I'm compelled to keep a careful distance. The impulse unsettles me. It's something between ethos and instinct, troubling the distinction between scientific objectivity and spiritual reverence. The roots are much finer here, and tinted with faint red. They are so deeply embedded inside this animal that, had an 18th-century artist rendered the scene, one could assume the ink roots were there to diagram the coyote's circulatory system—every vein and artery exploded for optimum legibility and analysis.

This coyote may have starved to a skeletal state just like that bear had. Just like most animals here in this cloistered wild probably had, without any local park rangers or fish and game wardens to put them out of their misery. It's a perfectly logical assumption to make. And yet, I don't buy it. There's something to the quality of the coyote's thinness. Something different from the bear's passive, ponderous decay. It isn't sunken. It's been shrunk. That bear had eaten itself from the inside. Looking at what remains of this coyote, though, I can't shake the sense that something else was feeding *from* it. And it won't have been the little opportunistic weeds peeking out from its ribs.

It's whatever's deployed all these roots.

A warning prickle on the back of my neck

rises to my right cheek. Phantom sensation coaxes my attention to the left, to the mummified offering cradled in the roots, to the half-consumed sacrifice, to the smaller plants, little weeds and bloomless wildflowers that spring from those once painful places where fear and hunger used to dwell.

Instincts that know only fight, flight, freeze, and fawn bid me to *fly*. Instead, I'm frozen in place, contemplating the answer to Leon's question: Why haven't the flowers evolved to bloom for us? Maybe that answer is actually quite basic. Basic enough to be *trite,* even... and yet so farfetched as to be fantastical.

Because, Professor Angelo, the flowers were too busy evolving to do something, *anything* else.

Crack.

I take a step back when the sound returns. A muffled, static crackle.

It's coming from the dead coyote's stomach. I don't breathe. I listen. Crackling white noise takes on form, but only in fragments. Broken pieces of a woman's voice rise from the hollow, desiccated sack before me.

"Dic—shun—men—nah—u—natur—phil—dee—er—wild—you—six—"

The crackling gets louder, consuming what little scraps of speech remained.

Recorded heavy breathing gives me the uncanny sense that this dead creature in front of me is breathing. I stare at its stomach to remind myself that it isn't—the way a child afraid of monsters in the closet forces himself to open it up and look inside in the hopes he might finally, *finally* manage a dreamless sleep.

Then, the woman trapped in the belly of the beast returns to plead. "I didn't know what they would do. I didn't *know*. I'm so *sorry*—" Breaths like sobs come next, making her voice fragile. Words break easily against the dead skin separating them from the air. "I would never, I would *never*—"

It stops.

A strained wheeze steers my attention to the coyote's throat. I could have sworn the poor thing was choking. Groans follow, muffled as if whatever's playing the recording is being digested more, making its way from the coyote's stomach to course deeper through the withered labyrinth of its intestines. A low growl, a high growl, a low growl. The strange pitch moves up and down, back and forth, getting faster and faster until it breaks apart into a wet, gurgling moan that I can't help but interpret as *relief*.

I reach to the knife holster at my hip to excise the device inside the coyote. I've got one hand braced on its ribs, the other ready to guide the knife in. My fingers trace the rough, papery belly, feeling it out. It crinkles. Bits of fur and skin flake off at my slightest touch. It isn't long before I feel a variance in texture, an inorganic shape that has no place in a—

"Shiloh?"

My grip on the knife is so tight I can't feel my

left hand. I fall on my ass in my scramble to get away. The voice says that name again, and I know it's him. It's Leon. I realize my right hand has moved to clasp my throat. I swallow hard against my palm, breathe in through my nose, and force my hand to relax.

The coyote growls from deep in its belly, and Leon's next words come in growls too. "Such a good boy." Every sound he makes lands in hot puffs of breath against my hair, ear, and neck. His gritted *"Fuck"* feels bitten into my shoulder, and I know he's close. His panting breaths come closer together, each punctuated with a sharp grunt. Every sound sketches more detail into the rhythm of his fucking. His voice is deeper still, rumbling from its hollow, dead auditorium. "Such a good boy—"

The tightness of my own fear edges the words that follow. For the first time, I hear Dr. Leon Angelo afraid—genuinely *terrified* when he says, "Shiloh?"

Raw *panic* follows. "Fuck!" Leon's voice disintegrates into urgent whispers, "Shiloh, there's—"

A *crickle-crack*. A series of barely-there sounds, like snow landing on your umbrella. A silk hood drawn past your ears. The soft *snap* of pruning a leaf.

Leon's final words come between choked sobs. "Oh *god!*" Reverb and distortion get louder, but so do Leon's panicked cries. Both are so loud, the coyote itself might just be screaming. Those screams break apart into dissonant streams of climax and terror before ending abruptly.

Silence sits heavily on my shoulders, pushing my side down to the ground. Realization punches me in the stomach, and I twist and wretch. I've just heard a man die. A man I know—*knew*. Intimately.

I struggle to wipe my mouth with a shaking hand.

Crickle-crickle-crackle.

Sound returns. I watch, not breathing as the ratty, chapped suede drum of the coyote's ribcage expands.

The coyote is *breathing in.*

Low, rumbling sounds swell from deep within the beast's steadily distending belly. I can smell its breath—sulphur and honey. Then, a voice far clearer, far louder than any of the others echoes before me as it licks its way into my ear. *"S—s—such a good boy-y-y-y-y-y-y-y."*

Okay, think. *Think.*

These vines I've been seeing throughout the wilderness are not vines. They're the aerial roots of some massive plant or network of plants that's managed to run highways through this place. Like a cloned forest of aspen, maybe, but not underground. Above it. An epiphyte, then. Carnivorous *and* parasitic? Multiple modes of feeding aren't unheard of. Venus flytraps are carnivorous, but they still photosynthesize. Adaptability means survivability, and only the most adaptable have made it through all these decades—*centuries* of environmental degradation. That coyote had not been buried. The roots had grown *down* to meet it. This organism, whatever it is, is feeding above ground.

My hypothesis guides my eyes upward. Directly counter to what so many other organisms would have done, these roots get thicker the higher they climb, shifting from the dusty browns of the earth to something richer. Redder. I follow their braided path up a pine tree where they merge into a single branch as thick as my arm. From there it spans the canopy to another tree, and another, and another. Using that line of dried-blood brown like a guide rail, I make my way through the forest, walking very slowly, letting myself find my footing before each careful step forward.

Ten minutes now I've been following that one root, and the heady smell of sweet sulphur has just gotten stronger. I've yet to see a single leaf. Either these roots are leading to some massive central organism, or it *has* no leaves. Why not? Nature may be on its last legs, but the sun isn't dead. Not yet. It burns plenty bright at this latitude, even with the canopy cover. So why not photosynthesize using its exposed roots? Why such inefficient use of surface? Maybe the conditions above ground recently spurred resource reallocation to the root system instead? But no, this is an epiphyte. I can tell from the silvery paper sheath the roots take on in places where there's less moisture to be found.

My apartment is packed with aerial roots just like that.

I stop where a length of pinky-mauve roots has broken from the main line and threaded their way down a tree, making their way back toward the earth. It's glossy—firm and plump to the touch. It can't be that the pinkish color is a result of dehydration. Still no trace of green to be found. How does it produce energy? Airborne particulates? Like some sort of above-ground filter feeder?

Slowly shaking my head, I stare at the mass of roots reaching to the ground in a curious, almost wicker-like structure roughly the size of myself. I can't help but pose my question aloud, my voice raspy and exhausted from coughing up bile. "How the fuck does it sustain itself?"

A crack of black runs up the center. Hollow? I force my fingers through, then hiss in pain. The cut on my wrist has opened again. I keep going, hands held together like a shovel blade, piercing the papery shell until I hit something with give. Something wet. Living, plump roots. Then, nothing. Using both arms, I part the crack as wide as it will go without damaging the roots. It takes my flashlight to see anything but black. I sweep light along the botanical cavern's insides, charting the space. The roots here are a far richer red than those crisscrossing the trees. They take on a glossy, fuchsia speckle that seems almost gaudy.

Sweat tingles on my scalp as a chill sweeps

over me. The shape the roots have formed themselves around isn't just the size of me. It's the *shape* of me. And on the ground beside a stick of pale wood, peeking above the loam, are the metal eyelets and weathered leather tongue of a hiking boot. A thin tendril of red root has slipped between the laces. Wedged inside some roots at knee height is a belt buckle, dull with patina. The wearer of these things is gone. Nothing remains of him but the form left behind by this orchid's loving embrace.

I only just heard a man die. Now, I am looking at the empty space left behind by a human body, long since consumed. With that recognition comes another—the recognition of what that length of pale wood actually is: a human femur. Degraded, partially disintegrated, but the shape is unmistakable. Craquelure covers every inch of it. Fine, rust-colored lines give way to deeper fractures where a red tendril is wound about it.

That vine twitches.

I take a step back, and it twitches again in some grotesque imitation of a lecherous, beckoning tongue. A come-hither finger that bids me do anything but. I wrinkle my nose against the stench rising from the human statue these roots have carved in relief. Sickly sweet, musky—a smell with the gut-punch of decay without the acrid bite. The headiness of musk but loftier. Floral. A red-wine tang, the bitter afterthought of tea left to steep then forgotten.

I tie my blue bandana around my face and all

I smell is my own dried blood. Though the respite doesn't last, even that small amount of sensory feedback keeps my head on straight long enough to back away from where my churning stomach tells me Leon Angelo died. At eye-level, I spot a glimmer of gold, deep in the hollow of the woven roots.

A fountain pen. And it's jutting from the eye cavity of a dusty, papier-mâché skull. Except it's not. I know it's not. That's what it looks like, though—papier-mâché—so that's what I keep telling myself it is to keep what's left of my stomach acid where it belongs. I manage it, even as the truth sits heavily on my chest. It's Leon's head, sucked dry by whatever's been feeding off what animals remain in this wilderness.

A wry laugh escapes me; I start at the sudden and very much unintended loudness of it. How can I not laugh? My freshman Philosophy T.A. told us we had to imagine Sisyphus happy. Didn't matter if he *actually was happy*—or so I'd been told when I asked.

Well, now I imagine the last animal in the Western Expanse happy. It occurs to me that said last animal is about to die in a cowboy hat with a bandana tied around his face, dressed like a fucking off-ramp strip-club highwayman or some FTM fetishist's wet fucking dream—so what I actually find is the last animal fucking *hysterical*.

But we've still got to imagine him *happy,* don't we?

Jesus fucking Christ.

Everybody was wrong about alcohol. It's sobriety that's going to kill me. I start laughing properly at that—so much, that I have to lift the point of my bandana to dab away a tear. The thing used to be navy, but it's changed. Not in a 'this has been stained in blood and dirt and worn to shit' sort of way. A 'this must be the color blue that shrimp can see' way.

"Well fuck me with an epiphyte," I say. "I'm *rolling* right now. I'm high on pretentious pervy professor… pmurder-r-r-r—" A laugh blows out my lips before I can get out the last word.

If whatever's gotten into my head had gotten into Val Rowan's head, it's affecting us *very* differently. Her journal hadn't exactly been lighthearted existential observations and alliterative comedic stylings. By the sounds of things on that recording, Leon had (to understate things severely) quite the bad trip.

Fuck, I *really* have got to stop laughing.

Maybe I've got some fucked-up tolerance or something? That does stop the laughing. All the better to run through the unofficial substance-use catalogue I keep in my long-term memory just for such a purpose. I keep a running list on my phone labeled FOR EMTS, but I haven't got that on me.

Well, darn.

It's getting cold again. I hadn't even realized it had been markedly warmer moments ago. I'm not laughing anymore. Now, there's just a hollow well in my gut where fear should be. I place a hand over my stomach and imagine little weeds poking their way through the spaces between my fingers. Sprouting little tendrils that circle the air in search of a landing place—a place to climb away from.

A voice treads over the vowels of my name, in the rhythm of my name. It's right here and distant all at once, like a song stuck in my head. It fades in and out, but always returns where it ought to have been had it never left.

"Or—on?"

Even in fragments, I recognize the name—that broken way of saying my name.

I'm still detoxing. She's here how maggots were here. Hell, maybe this fucked-up, impossible plant I've been tracking is just another part of it.

"Orion."

She doesn't stumble on my name anymore. Or is it just my desperation to hear her say my name, whole and entire and unbroken, that makes it so?

I stumble to the right like I'm carrying an uneven load. But I'm not. I'm not wearing my pack anymore. I don't remember taking it off.

Something warm and gentle but firm rests between my shoulder blades.

"Orion," she whispers, words frayed with quiet amazement. "It's... God, it's been ages."

"Yeah," I scoff. "And whose fault is that?" I step away from the weight at my back, but it never leaves me.

"Mine, sweetheart. All mine." A short,

bracing sigh and then, "I am so, so sorry. I have a lot of regrets but none wounds me like my regret for treating you like"—*like nothing we shared together ever meant anything?*—"like nothing we shared together ever meant anything"—*like you never gave a damn about me?*—"like I never gave a damn about you"—*like I'm disposable?*—"like you're disposable."

What's there to be sorry about? I am disposable.

The hand between my shoulder blades slides up to my shoulder to give it a squeeze. "No, you're not."

I know I should walk away, but I'm turning to face her instead. Thick, curly black hair tickles my nose when she kisses my cheek. She smells how she always did. Like the coconut oil she uses for just about everything, the sanitizing chemicals she uses for her work, and my teatree shampoo which she never admits to using. I close my eyes, and she kisses my temple, the side of my neck... just below my jaw, where it makes me melt every time.

When she cups my face to brush a thumb across my cheek, I realize I'm crying. I haven't cried in ages. Not since starting testosterone. Not even when she left.

The illusion of the maggots didn't last more than a few minutes.

Zoë feels more real, more present now than she ever did.

I open my eyes.

Zoë. Her bare, olive skin is dotted with

freckles and tattoos. My eyes move across them like stepping stones, pausing to rest on the softness of her stomach… the treble-clef curve of her hip, the dimples just below the lushest part of her. Inner thighs jiggle when she moves her hand between her legs and starts sliding her fingers through fine, curling hair. She pushes lower, then deeper with a quiet gasp. Her gently thrusting hand makes a sound so slick, it gives the air a taste. A little sweet, a little sharp, with just the edge of something metallic.

Zoë herself presses against me, large breasts swelling against my own flat chest. Between bites on my throat, she begs me how she used to when we were still M.A. students—when she still wanted me badly enough to risk getting caught and never being taken seriously in that department again. When she used to lock our shared office door between seminars, straddle my lap and start grinding against me. "Please, *please* will you make me come? Fuck, I need you so bad, Orion."

Only, she never called me "Orion" then.

She didn't even always call me "Orion" *after.*

Fuck, this hurts. It isn't real. I know it isn't real. But knowing that doesn't make me want to draw my knife from my belt and *just fucking die already* any less. Back in California, the *real* Zöe won't be having guilt-induced benders or regretful nightmares about me. Why would she? She's got just what she always wanted but would never admit to wanting out loud: some biological offspring to raise with their biological father. My throat's tight. I hate how weak it makes my voice sound when I say, "If it's all the same to you, I preferred the episode with the maggots."

I hate that I'm crying again even more. Quietly, yes, but tears are definitely flooding my cheeks, making me feel feverish. Too hot on the surface, too cold in my bones. I'm just so fucking mad—at Zoë, but mostly myself. I'm mad that *this*, of all the fucked-up shit I've been through this past decade, is what finally triggered tears.

I was wrong. This is like the maggots. Only in this nightmare vision, the parasite is feeding off the hundreds of little nicks, scrapes, and cuts I racked up over the years, throwing myself at the feet of people who only want me when I don't want myself.

"Fuck, Zo," I barely manage past my fist-tight throat. "I wish I could just fucking *hate you*."

Zoë considers me with big, green eyes. She wipes my tears away with a finger that's as warm as it should be, but too firm. Too smooth. The touch feels like it's coming from something only about half its size in diameter. It tickles more than soothes. Itches. She sticks that finger in her mouth, considering. There's nothing sexual or romantic about the gesture.

Just *curious*.

Then, she places a hand on my lower back. Only, it's far bigger, far firmer than her hand—any human hand should be. Above her brow, one tendril of black hair extends, uncurls, then stretches into space a moment before relaxing back into a spool.

Her other hand grips my injured one tightly enough to unknit what little skin I've managed to heal, and I hiss in pain.

"So, what's the play here?" I ask, wincing. "You trigger some flood of neurochemicals—pheromones or some DMT-adjacent compound, maybe—lure me into... what, taking off all my clothes so your digestive enzymes don't choke on my cowboy hat? If so, I gotta say: botanists really wasted the name 'Venus flytrap' on something that doesn't use some pseudo version of Pouyannian mimicry to lure in prey."

Zoë frowns. Or, pouts, actually. Her eyes are glistening, too—not so much like a woman about to cry as a doll caught in the rain. I put my hands on her bare shoulders and say, "I'm five foot eight inches tall. Zoë is five foot nine. This—" I pause to give her naked body a sweeping look. "Is five foot five, tops. Which is funny, because I used to fantasize what it would be like if she were shorter than me... how good that would make me feel. So..."—I tip my hat—"well played, ma'am. That's a real—"

Her mouth is against mine, warm and wet—tongue already forcing its way inside before I can so much as pull away. I hold her by the shoulders at arm's length and narrow my eyes. "The fuck is that? You trying to get a read on my DNA or something? Figure out if you want to kill me or recruit me like some fucking *ant*?" I tilt my head, conceding, "Admittedly, if that *is* what's happening here, it is objectively rad as hell. I can't even be mad about it—just, like, as a botanist."

My hands push closer together when Zoë's skin gives, her whole body crumpling like a neglected soufflé.

And there it is.

A flower. Red. Deep red. The red of a wound. Of meat. Freckles of black, like the threat of fainting on the field of vision. Then, that blackness floods into the flower's center, sucking my gaze down with it. This is where that vast labyrinth of aerial roots has been leading to. This massive, woman-sized orchid. It's a network so sprawling, and here so tightly woven that the huge tree supporting it has been eclipsed completely by rose-tinted roots.

If the tree is even still there at all. What tree could survive a permanent eclipse?

How ancient must this plant be? Staring into the black whorl at the flower's center, my consciousness strains with the effort of not ripping itself in half. Behind me, is the sense of being watched. Laid out in front of me, is the knowledge that I am beholding something far too large for me to comprehend in anything but fragments. This leviathan of the forest grows on a scale so much larger than me in every dimension.

And it's staring at me.

It sees me watching *it*.

Raw red petals ripple like thick flesh that's just been *smacked*. Lateral sepals spread wider like inviting thighs, exposing the pink tint of their undersides. A plump, freckled labellum licks its way into the central hole that must lead into the column of its nectary tube. As I keep staring into it, I can make out fat sacks of black glistening within. One drips pearly liquid; its splash sends out a sweet, heady perfume that forces my mouth to water.

Digestive enzymes? Or something else? If this is indeed an orchid—and it certainly looks to be an orchid—carnivory isn't something it's built for. While this is certainly something of an outlier in a lot of ways, there is nothing about its basic structure that says anything but *Orchidaceae*. I shift my weight and bite back a groan—now very, very aware that I am very, very hard. I scoff. "You have got to be fucking kidding me."

Pouyannian mimicry.

Orchidaceae induce pseudo-copulation with their pollinators by imitating the females of the pollinating species. *Drakaea isolata,* the Lonely Hammer Orchid, imitates the flightless female of the Thynnid wasp species: right down to her shape, her color, her positioning relative to the ground, even her pheromones. The male spots it. Then, while the male wasp fucks the flower, its hinged stem springs back, coating the wasp in its pollen— spreading orchid genetic material each time it gets horny. Hell, male wasps have been observed flying right past real female wasps to copulate with the orchid instead. The prevailing assumption being that the orchid has managed to synthesize a maximally intoxicating female wasp pheromone.

Any resulting fidelity of pollinators to their orchids, so far as most scientists are concerned, supports this view. All of these wasps had all been unknowing dupes in some fucked-up floral game—too stupid to tell a flower apart from another of their own kind. Otherwise, why would they waste their energies fucking something they couldn't impregnate?

My dissertation disagreed.

If a male wasp was never faithful to the female wasps it did manage to fuck, why would it be faithful to a flower it had mistaken for one? It wouldn't. Unless it knew the orchid was *different*.

Because the orchid told it so.

I discussed mimicry at length in my thesis, but only Pouyannian mimicry got its own chapter: on the uncanny as a mode of playfulness. Leon, still my advisor then, had asked if my particular affinity for Pouyannian mimicry—"sexual deception" was the term he'd used—came from "personal experience." The implication being that I lured homosexual men into my bed under false pretenses, just so they'd *pollinate me*.

Which, considering just how many times I'd told some cis guy I didn't bottom only for him to "accidentally" slide it in (and *not* in my *ass*)—and the fact that I'm far from alone—I'd say it's not the *trans* men participating in sexual deception. Maybe cis assholes just emit some sort of alkanes that induce me into losing any and all standards, self-regard, and desire for pleasure. I give a derisive snort—mostly aimed at myself.

Did this orchid adapt to neurochemically manipulate mammalian behavior? How? If this plant is deploying sexed-up hallucinations in a bid to induce pseudo-copulation, it may not be for *pollination*. Am I staring into the imaginary eyes of an orchid, a flower looking to pollinate? Or a *Venus flytrap*, a predator looking to feed?

Carnivory is found in those plants braving the harshest and least forgiving environments. Adapted to sparse conditions by producing enzymes capable of making meat bioavailable. Something they'd usually have to rely on fungi or animal excretion for a digestive assist. Florida may be an unforgiving environment for me, but not for an orchid. At least, not before the loss of so much animal life resulted in this mass, trophic cascade. Humanity will probably die off well before it can fully understand just how far those consequences ripple.

But why reveal the trick now?

The same reason the magician's assistant emerges from the box with her legs on: the applause. Because it's all a performance, and a performance goes both ways. Always. This plant has sampled my saliva, my blood, my tears. It's judged me the way a myrmecophyte reads insect saliva to determine whom to feed and whom to poison. Leon, I expect, had been judged a predator—a threat to be eliminated. Val Rowan, then, was recruited.

And me? It's hard to say. But the rich tan the orchid's fluttering petals are taking on lends me to suspect I've been selected for neither of those.

Life and death situations aside, I feel this really validates my dissertation's core argument.

The blossom is changing. But this isn't a hallucination projected by my own mind. The orchid itself is shifting form to take on human, feminine shapes. Sepals extend into legs, lateral petals reach out into arms, plump labellum curl into a slowly writhing torso. Creases form at the sides of full breasts when she moves her arms down her soft stomach, like she's sculpting and discovering herself all at once. A featureless head rises from the stem, roots melting into soft, long black hair. The mouth forms first, wide and smirking. Next is the nose, cheeks. Eyes the same shape, same color as mine look at me through long black lashes. Every blink makes the freckles across her nose shimmer with the ghost of her natural, pinot noir red. Each of those freckles mirrors my own.

It's Aurora Maya Armijo. Ten years ago, I looked like that. Less than ten, even. This was what the world saw before I'd even started cutting my hair short, let alone started testosterone. Except, I didn't look like that. Not exactly. This is far from a perfect copy. Because this isn't the idealized projection of my mind. This is real. *Here.* Any animal in this forest would see what I'm seeing. The imperfect blend of brown skin with plant. It isn't clumsy like an amateur makeup job. Looking at it's more like looking at an impressionistic painting, walking closer to see the sculpture in the paint strokes, walking back again to see a scene more lifelike than any photograph.

This has artistry. I stare at the deep tan flesh creasing where her thigh meets her stomach long enough and I see flushed, swollen petals—stitched together like a day-old cut. Something even my tongue could rip open. She opens her thighs how a morning glory opens its petals. Building anticipation before blooming all at once. The lingering immediacy of a poem. Practical, yet so, so grotesquely and gloriously baroque.

Weren't all flowers once?

Between the orchid's thighs is her nectary. Has to be. She rakes her fingers through the fine hairs covering her plump vulva—human in color but edged with red, stiffer than a person's would be. They're far more like the orchid's own wooly labellar hairs: designed to sense the barest kiss of motion to... trigger what exactly?

Shutting the trap?

Swallowing the fly so slowly it takes weeks to die?

But this isn't a Venus fly trap, and the stigma turned clit she's tracing slow circles around now isn't an organ for feeding. It's for reproducing. For pleasure. *Especially* for pleasure. The air around her hums with it.

I watch her touch herself—so unbothered, so unconscious, so *painless*—with envy. Back then, I'd masturbated for relief when I really needed to, like cracking a joint. Always relying on tools to get it done quickly with minimal hand-to-genital contact. No medium, no intervening mechanism separates her pleasure from my body now. Only air. Time.

I tug off my shirt, kneel between her spread legs, reach out, and touch my former self. Her hand guides mine lower, to slip between wet lips that shift between plant and animal in my mind. When I feel just how wet she is there, how warm, how responsive, I'm not so sure the distinction between plant and animal makes sense anymore. All I see is pink. But not the pink of a blush. The thick, shining pink of a tongue after it's been bit. The flesh beneath the fingernail, exposed. The wet sheath containing an organ. It is a blush, all right. Just a blush ripped open and turned inside-out, displayed for what it really is. *Meat.*

A blush with teeth.

The orchid's knees tilt back, and I let my weight fall against her, delighting in the contrast between us: the generous give of her body against my flat, solid torso. Her smile is all the more smirk-like when her chin tilts back. I kiss her exposed throat, her neck, placing lingering, sucking kisses just beneath her jaw where it always did and always will make me melt—*whoever* I am.

I don't bother turning to see just what is tugging off my shoes, pants, and underwear. Couldn't, even if I wanted to, once fingers as flexible as vines twine through my hair and tug me higher, bringing my mouth to her grinning one. She tastes like nothing but wetness and warmth. I laugh lightly against her lips when realization hits: Of course she doesn't taste like anything to me. All her mouth tastes like is *mine.*

The thought of tasting the rest of her makes my mouth water anyway. She must know it; her grin tickles my lips. Vine-like hands let me go, and I kiss my way down, pausing to nibble her collarbone. Using my tongue, I trace the tattoos she lacks—anointing her with sacred images. The female, seed-bearing branch of the gingko tree dips to the swell of her left breast. Her right breast ripples and trembles as she does. She sinks deeper into the earth, legs closing around me when I complete the branch, licking its male pollen-producing branch onto her right breast. I kiss the last leaf onto her shoulder.

Hands guide me where she wants me, lower. I suck a dark nipple into my mouth, and she squirms beneath me, letting out something between a rustling-leaf giggle and a creaking-wood moan each time I use my tongue—a proper moan when I use my teeth.

When my chin is brushed by the hairs crowning her vulva, the change in the air is palpable. Electric. Her body's hotter now. Once I place a feather kiss to the plush softness beneath her navel, and another to the crease of her thigh, her whole body trembles. Bejeweled reds and purples wash over her skin in liquid flashes like a squid, oscillating between bloody fuchsia and brown.

The air cycles through a rainbow of scents, too. The heaviest scent, the one making my mouth water, comes from between her legs. Nectar drips onto my hand. It's a pearlescent violet. Sweet smelling. Some species exude nectar to tempt a symbiont. Others to lure in, and then eliminate a threat.

She's watching me carefully. I lick my fingers and grin at the brief flash of lilac pink that lights up her chest, throat, and cheeks.

Good lord, I'm *drooling*. I wipe my forearm across my chin. Either the dripping wet, pulsing redness between her legs just looks that good, or my brain is swimming in semiochemical soup right now.

I could not care fucking less.

I dip back down to taste her properly, waiting for my jaw to glue shut like so many pre-twenty-first-century caterpillars. She tastes how I imagine non-synthetic honey must have tasted. Floral. Sweet. With the unmistakable thrum of something animal.

I lick her again, and petals quiver against my ears. My tongue pushes against those places I knew would get me off fastest, get it over with, but I take my time. Her inner lips cycle through a bouquet of colors I've only seen in photographs, but I can identify them all. Verbena. Iris. Monkshood. Larkspur.

I chase the deeper, redder shades of violet—repeating the gentle sucks that make her flush in a field of salvia and sweet pea, the hard licks that have fingers raking down my back and vines tugging at my hair.

Just when I think we might reach something like a climax, something starts growing beneath my lips. Her clit swells, lengthens, turning the same bruised red as her insides. It's even longer than my T-dick now. I look up to find arms spread wide. Invitation.

I take it.

Her legs guide my pelvis against hers. My dick slides against her with a wet sound, and I bite back a groan. She's so warm, so wet, it almost feels like I could actually fuck her—with my own body. I can't. Not how I want to.

The orchid Aurora is studying me. She asks, "Do you hate me?"

"No," I tell her, smiling when I realize it's true. "And I don't want to."

This seems to confuse her a moment. But then she smiles, thighs wrapping around my waist, heels pressing into my ass to pull me closer. I keep my eyes locked on hers while I rock against her, watching her brown skin shift between shades of violet with every low groan of mine.

She holds me tighter, locking me in place. Something sucks onto my dick. I freeze, try to break away, but she's too strong. I hiss out, "*Fuck!*" when whatever it is *pierces* its way inside the most sensitive part of me. Any pain is barely a whimper against the pleasure of it. Maybe my masochism goes way deeper than I thought. But maybe, just maybe, my nerves recognize that the hole being drilled into me is one that's *meant* to be there.

The roots pinning me down relax, and I pull back—then *moan*. I can *feel* her. I *really feel* myself sliding out of her, feel the clench of her, the drag of her insides on my dick. Again, she's looking at me with that careful, studious face.

I push into her, and she smiles around a laughing moan. Her legs are back on mine, guiding me to fuck her where and how she wants. She wants it deep. Hard. Just how I would have wanted to be fucked if the very thought hadn't made my insides squirm.

Heat blossoms at the base of my dick, tugging behind my navel and sending shocks down my thighs. Legs yank me close with a *smack* and I pant out a laugh. I fuck her deep enough to hear my balls smack against her again. It hurts but I don't care because hurt means I can feel it. It's real—sprung up from the broken pieces of me, finally regrown. Healed. I feel my dick, tip to base and deeper. The roots of it reach deep inside me, holding fast to my nerves with the surest connection to the neurons that blaze *God, yes, fuck—just like that* and *More, please, more—*

She kisses me when I come, swallowing my broken moan.

I lay my head against her, listening to the sounds her body doesn't make. The stomach I worked so hard to chisel away into something hard, less accommodating, welcomes my resting cheek. My cheek slides easily against her breast and sternum. She isn't sweating. I'm crying again. I'm still inside her because I'm terrified to pull out—terrified to find out what doesn't come away with me. It isn't just silent tears anymore; I'm crying, really fucking sobbing now.

The orchid who looks how I could never bear to holds me closer.

I don't stop crying. I don't stop any of it.

Four Weeks Later...

The president's palace—one of them—is a
shockingly tasteful building that would look at
home on the rocky, ocean-side cliffs of southern
Spain. Except it's in northern Florida, on the sandy
flat beaches on the wrong side of the Atlantic.

Two armed guards lead me into an airy
sitting room lined in Moroccan tile. The eastern and
southern walls are open archways that look out onto
the sea, framed in billowing, sheer violet silk. The
breeze is so strong right now, the curtains seem to
be reaching for me.

My distant benefactor—the president's
wife—enters from one of these archways, dressed in
white organza just as dramatic as her curtains. Her
hair is platinum blonde, face as carefully painted as
the thousand tiles bordering the ceiling. She smiles
at me with a stiff, glossy pink mouth.

All I can think is: this is what *Great
Expectations* would be like if it had been recast with
D-list country/western stars.

The older of the guards accompanying me
scowls when I don't take off my cowboy hat. For the
sake of his blood pressure, I give it a tilt in her
direction and say, "Madam."

"Dr. Armijo," Isolde says, giving it the
tongue-heavy flair more at home in Spain than
Mexico. She dismisses the guard with a pointed look

and a jerk of her pointy chin. Then she graces me with a smile, arm sweeping me toward a turquoise chaise before sitting in the plush emerald chair opposite.

"Well!" she says, clapping her hands to her thighs. "You survived!"

I laugh lightly, cross my left leg on my right knee, and sling an arm behind me. I shift in the seat to stop the edge of this thing from squishing my balls. "You seem surprised."

Isolde's face settles, looking serious. "Happily so, I assure you."

I shrug. *If you say so, lady.* When she doesn't seem capable of doing anything other than staring at me, I arch an eyebrow at her. "So... now what? You got my write-up, yes? Don't know what you think I've got to add."

She huffs a laugh. "Plenty, I'm sure."

"Listen, ma'am," I tell her. "It's been a real weird time for me. If you could just shoot straight, I'd be awfully grateful."

Her thin-lipped smile looks almost grateful. "Alright," she says, "you survived."

"So they tell me."

"They did not."

"Dr. Angelo, no, but I thought Dr. Rowan had—"

"My daughter did not survive. She disappeared in that wilderness four years ago. Nobody survived—not for long, at least—since. Why? Why you? Why did you survive, Dr. Armijo?"

Interesting way to phrase the question: not *how* did you survive. *Why* did you survive. "Don't know," I say. "Maybe I've just got more experience doing it."

"Surviving?"

That was what I'd meant. Even so, I find myself humming, considering before correcting, "Navigating emptiness."

"Ah. *Horror vacui,*" she quotes sagely. "The horror of a vacuum. We learned it from nature."

I shrug. "Maybe. I'm not so sure it's true that nature abhors a vacuum. At least, the expression's not as true as it *could* be."

"Oh?" she asks. "And what expression would be truer to nature?"

I consider a moment, then answer, "*Cupiditas implendi.*"

A bright, baffled laugh. "Something about desire? I confess my Latin isn't as good as yours."

"Hm. Guess not." I stand and say, "If that's all, I've got to get going. I can hear my research calling me."

"Yes," she says slowly, narrowing her eyes. "I expect you can. In that case, I will let you go, Dr. Armijo."

I tilt my hat, say, "Ma'am," and show myself out.

Why won't the flowers bloom for us, Leon?

We never asked them.

Well... you didn't.

I turn over the Latin phrase I gave my bizarre

benefactor. Might just be a book title there.

Cupiditas Implendi: *Nature Loves to Fill a Hole.*

There are far more important names to be worked out than book titles. I'll have to ask her what she thinks of *Ophrys eurydicanthus.* Honestly, I'm tempted to scrap the Ophrys genus entirely. Plant classification has been sex-based for centuries, ever since Linnaeus decided reproductive organs are the distinguishing trait *par excellence.* "Female" reproductive organs here make this a violet, "Male" reproductive organs there make that an orchid or a rose. Flowers and I have got that in common, really....

Everybody always wants to know how it *fucks.*

Nobody ever thinks to ask how it *feeds.*

I love you as certain dark things are to be loved,

in secret, between the shadow and the soul.

I love you as the plant that never blooms

but carries in itself the light of hidden flowers;

thanks to your love a certain solid fragrance,

risen from the earth, lives darkly in my body.

Pablo Neruda, "XVII"

Acknowledgements

In 2024, four disparate-yet-related things happened to me. (1) Trump was reelected, so I got jacked on epiphytes. (2) I wound up in the ER. Twice. Don't worry about it. (1B) Okay, circling back to that because I'm sensing some puzzlement here: I exorcised much of my post-election angst into pumping iron while listening to audiobooks about orchids. (3) I fell in love. (4—hm, wait a sec. 2B) I'm basically fine, seriously. I wrote the insurance company a very strongly worded letter (with an extensive bibliography—by their standards, not mine) and now it's fine—by my standards, not those of a reasonable person. (4—actually, no: 1C) *Okay.* See what happened was I was so *&#^*@#&^$ inside all the time, but I was also way *too tired* to do something so, well, *tiresome* as relapse, so I just spent 6 hours a week lifting weights to the unsoothing lullaby that is floral nonfiction, steadily blooming into the botanically swole man you don't see before you.

And no, *actually,* I am not deflecting from (4). Maybe *you're* deflecting from (4).

Okay, fine. I'll tell you what you want to know.

The Light Eaters by Zoë Schlanger and *Orchid: A Cultural History* by Jim Endersby. Those were the two books I read mid-squat. Fascinating books, both of them—really almost successfully distracted my imagination from The Horrors. Consider those two authors acknowledged, please. Also consider acknowledging the little ghosts of Little Ghosts Books who decided my idea was worth pitching, my pitch worth soliciting, and my beefy, evasive ass worth publishing. Their willingness to not only tolerate but reward my excessively wordy bullshit is truly ~~enabling~~ touching. Finally, shout out to two dear friends in the high desert, Mel and Twig, for supporting me and my budding story. Both made very convincing " :o " faces and "ooOooo" sounds as I went off in a Santa Fe diner while eating something sad and pureed from a cup instead of the bacon bison chile burger I actually wanted so as not to wind up back in the ER for another experience so fucked up I had to write a horror story about it.

Love,
Elijah

About the Author

ELIJAH B. WILDER is a writer of speculative stories—often haunted, usually Queer, and almost always containing far more puns than can reasonably be considered "actually funny." His Ph.D. is in nothing remotely botanical, but he does have ultra-specific knowledge about plant reproduction and feels the need to make this everybody else's problem. He is a card-carrying Trans Man™ and has been known to keep an orchid alive for entire week at a time. His grim fantasy HEREAFTER LIES: R.I.P. is available, probably.

About Little Ghosts Books:

Little Ghosts Books is a horror bookstore and small press established in Toronto, Canada in 2022, with a vision to showcase indie horror from diverse voices.

Through our publishing imprint and physical space, we hope to connect readers, horror lovers, authors, and folks of all backgrounds.

Find out what we already know:
A Good Story Will Haunt You.

FOLLOW LITTLE GHOSTS:
@littleghostsbooks
www.littleghostsbooks.com
littleghostsbooks on Substack

www.ingramcontent.com/pod-product-compliance
Lightning Source LLC
Chambersburg PA
CBHW011053130726
47906CB00010B/1053

9 781069 541505